"Which is my room?" Jenneth asked

There was a long pause before Luke said evenly, "It is customary for the bride and groom to share a room."

She withstood his gaze for as long as she could and then whispered unbelievingly, "Why? For convention? After all, we both know that it isn't because you..."

Inexplicably, she couldn't utter the final denouncing words. Why was it so difficult to say "it isn't because you desire me"? After all, it was the truth.

"What is it we both know, Jenneth?" he asked her softly, as he walked toward her. "What were you going to say? That I don't want you?"

His look made her stomach quiver and she felt a rush of heat course through her body. "Are you really so blind?" he asked mockingly.

PENNY JORDAN was constantly in trouble in school because of her inability to stop daydreaming—especially during French lessons. In her teens she was an avid romance reader, although it didn't occur to her to try writing one herself until she was older. "My first half-dozen attempts ended up ingloriously," she remembers, "but I persevered, and one manuscript was finished." She plucked up the courage to send it to a publisher, convinced her book would be rejected. It wasn't, and the rest is history! Penny is married and lives in Cheshire.

Penny Jordan's striking mainstream novel, *Power Play*, quickly became a *New York Times* bestseller. She followed that success with *Silver*, a story of ambition, passion and intrigue.

Watch for Penny's latest blockbuster, *The Hidden Years*, available in October wherever paperback books are sold.

Books by Penny Jordan

Don't miss any of our special offers. Write to us at the following address for information on our newest releases.

Harlequin Reader Service
P.O. Box 1397, Buffalo, NY 14240
Canadian address: P.O. Box 603,
Fort Erie, Ont. L2A 5X3

PENNY JORDAN

bitter betrayal

Harlequin Books

TORONTO • NEW YORK • LONDON
AMSTERDAM • PARIS • SYDNEY • HAMBURG
STOCKHOLM • ATHENS • TOKYO • MILAN

Harlequin Presents first edition June 1991
ISBN 0-373-11369-2

Original hardcover edition published in 1989
by Mills & Boon Limited

BITTER BETRAYAL

CHAPTER ONE

'YOU'RE doing what?' Jenneth asked her oldest and closest friend in astonishment, almost unable to believe what she was hearing, despite the crystal clarity of Louise's excited voice.

'Married. You know...to have and to hold, et cetera et cetera... A mortgage...kids...the whole bit,' Louise repeated obligingly, while Jenneth's astonishment almost hummed along the telephone wire from York to London.

Jenneth clutched the receiver and said protestingly, 'But you've always sworn you'd *never* marry! You wanted to be independent. You...'

'That was before I met George,' Louise told her unrepentantly.

George! Jenneth almost boggled, not just at the thought of her high-flying, career-orientated girlfriend getting married, but at the thought of her marrying a man called George... Had she ever been asked to stretch her imagination to the almost impossible lengths of visualising Louise getting married, she would have believed it would be to someone with a far more exotic name than George...

Sighing faintly, she ignored her cooling cup of coffee and the fact that unless she terminated her telephone call right now she was never going to get the preliminary sketches for the McGrath mural finished by lunchtime, and said severely, 'You never said anything two months ago when we met for lunch.'

'I hadn't met him then,' said Louise simply, and then added quickly, 'Look, Jen, I want you to be there...on the day, I mean. We're getting married in three weeks' time, at home, in the village church. We're having the whole bit...George says we might as well, since neither of us will get the chance again. I can't wait for you to meet him. I wish we could get together before the wedding, but George is going to be away in Japan on business...'

She chuckled richly as she heard Jenneth saying in a faint voice, 'I don't believe I'm hearing any of this.'

They had virtually grown up together and had been close friends all their lives, living in the same small village, going to the same school, and even later on to the same university, and then Jenneth's parents had moved further north and she had gone with them, eventually setting up her existing small studio in the barn attached to her parents' house outside York, while Louise had found herself a job in London in the frenetic world of advertising.

That had been seven years ago. Now Louise had her own agency, while Jenneth had developed her artistic talents to the point where she was greatly in demand locally for the murals which had become her speciality. In addition she had a half-share in a small private gallery in York itself. She and Louise had never totally lost touch, but these days it was impossible for them to meet as often as both of them would have wished.

Jenneth's parents had been killed just after their move to the north, leaving Jenneth solely responsible for the welfare of her then pre-teenage twin brothers...

There had been times when they had been a heavy responsibility indeed, but the knowledge that her parents would have wanted them all to stay together, coupled with her own deep-rooted sense of duty and responsibility, had helped her through the worst of the bad times.

The twins had now just finished their last year at school, two tall fair-haired males who towered over her and at times almost swamped her with their fierce protectiveness towards her...

Well knowing why Jenneth hadn't given her an instantaneous response, Louise coaxed, 'Promise me you're going to be there. It's three weeks on Saturday. I'm not having any bridesmaids or anything like that, but I need you there, Jenneth... Seriously...'

There was just enough emotion in her voice for Jenneth to check the automatic refusal hovering on her lips, and Louise took advantage of her silence to add, 'I've booked you a room at the Feathers. Can't put you up at home, I'm afraid, the place will be brimming over with aged aunts and the like, although Mum and Dad are both looking forward to seeing you...'

'I don't know if I can make it, Louise,' Jenneth told her, staring unseeingly out of her studio window and into the verdant jungle of the house's back garden.

The house had a very large garden, far too large for her to manage, but she and the twins loved their home. The barn which she had had converted into her studio was ideal for her work, and none of them had wanted to move after the accident, although once the boys were at university... They had been arguing about it ever since Christmas, Kit and Nick both determined to persuade her not to put the house up for sale, even though she had pointed out to them that once they were at university it would be far too large for her, and that the money from the sale would realise lump-sum nest-eggs for them when they set out into the world.

Her hand clenched around the receiver, her palm suddenly sticky with tension, with all that she wanted to say and could not—partly because the words simply refused to be spoken, clogging her throat, and partly because of the old habit of ingrained reticence. So unlike Louise's outgoing, frank inability to do anything other than say what she was thinking and feeling.

She did it now, taking a deep breath that Jenneth could actually hear, and then, while a bird soared and sang overhead outside, she heard her friend saying softly, 'Luke won't be there, if that's what's worrying you. He's away in the States on business. Please say you'll be there.'

Although she hadn't moved, Jenneth experienced a familiar dizzying, frightening sensation of fear-induced panic. She hesitated, wanting to find the right words to preserve her dignity... to deny the importance of what Louise was saying, to break through her own reserve and pour out from her heart the feelings which she herself had made taboo between them, eight years ago, by refusing to discuss them with anyone... especially not with Luke's cousin, even if she *was* also her own best friend.

'Jenneth, please...' Louise wheedled, and as the spectre of Luke rose mockingly to taunt her with her own cowardice she took a deep breath and said huskily,

'Yes, of course I will...'

They talked for another few minutes, or rather Louise talked and Jenneth listened, while she waited for her agitated heartbeat to slow down to normal and the tension to leave her body. As she listened, she wondered what she would have said had Luke been attending the wedding...and then, a little cynically, asked herself silently if Louise would have invited her had that been the case.

Of course she would, she told herself after they had said their goodbyes and she had replaced the receiver.

Although she had never been able to hide from her friend how much she dreaded the thought of being brought face to face with Luke, thankfully Louise had spent the six-month span of Jenneth's engagement to him studying abroad, and, being Louise, had sought no other explanation for the ending of that engagement other than the one Jenneth gave her, which was simply that they had both realised it was a mistake.

In the early days, when self-hatred had burned her like acid, she had privately blamed herself for her parents' death, knowing that their move to York had in part been prompted by their concern for her, but the years had eased that particular torment a little. There were other torments, though, that would never go away. It was useless telling herself that she was far too sensitive. The anguish of hearing from Luke's own lips that, while professing to love her, he had been seeing someone else and that that someone else was now carrying his child, was something she could never eradicate.

It was burned into her as though by torture; and, like any victim of such cruelty, she carried the brand of Luke's rejection of her in her soul—deep within her. Behind the calm, pleasant mask she wore for the world there lived a very different person indeed. Some people thought of her as aloof, claiming that her manner matched the coolness of her Nordic fall of wheat-blonde hair and the unfathomable greyness of her dark-lashed eyes.

In response she possessed an aura of calm which had been hard won and which she had learned to project to protect herself. When she moved it was with contained, controlled movements that made those who were baffled and infuriated by the distance at which she held them condemn her as withdrawn and emotionless, not realising that the reverse was the truth, and that it was to protect herself from her own acute vulnerability that she had had to learn the savagely painful lesson of concealing her real feelings.

Now what had at first been a disguise she had assumed for the sake of her pride had become an intrinsic part of her, to such an extent that it was only Louise and the twins who were still able to penetrate the façade of remoteness.

Over the years she had learned to temper her own feelings of rejection and grief with the received wisdom of experience and age, telling herself that the relationship between her and Luke would never have worked; that at twenty-one she had been far too immature, and that the engagement would have petered out anyway, given time.

What still did have the power to confuse her was why Luke had got engaged to her in the first place. Eight years her and Louise's senior, he had seemed to her a god-like creature set on the heights, way, way above her touch. All through her teens she was in turn giddy, shy, self-conscious and finally spell-bound in his presence, whenever school holidays threw the three of them together and Luke, who was away first at boarding-school, then at university, and finally lecturing abroad, came home.

His family, unlike hers, had been part of the village for several generations. His father was the local GP, and his mother, despite the fact that the crippling multiple sclerosis from which she suffered had weakened her health appallingly, took as active a role as she could in village affairs. Tender-hearted, and popular with everyone who knew her, she had gently approved of Luke's engagement to Jenneth.

Luke had loved his mother very deeply, treating her with the same protective concern with which the twins were now trying to suffocate Jenneth, although in Luke's mother's case she had far more need of that protectiveness than Jenneth.

In looks, however, Luke took after his father; he had his tall, very male leanness, and his thick, dark hair.

Louise had once shocked her by telling her that her mother's brother, Luke's father, had had something of a reputation with their sex, before he'd met and married Luke's mother. She had been a local heiress, and Luke's father had fallen in love with her and married her despite the opposition of her family. Jenneth had always thought it a very romantic story.

Now Luke's mother was dead. She had died several months after Luke had married...

Automatically Jenneth ducked her head, letting her hair swing forward to conceal her expression, even though there was no one there to see her. Even now, the thought of that agonising time when Luke had told her so clinically and coldly, as though every word he said to her had to be weighed and accounted for, that he was marrying someone else— a someone else who had already conceived his child—still had an overpowering and disturbing effect on her.

How often had she told herself that thousands of young women were rejected by men they thought loved them, and that they, unlike her, went on to form other, lasting, less destructive relationships without any difficulty at all? How often had she chided herself both verbally and mentally for behaving like a wilting Victorian heroine, falling into what used to euphemistically be called a 'decline' because her world had been turned upside-down by the discovery that the love she had thought its surest foundation had never really existed?

Oh, outwardly she had done all the right things: listened to Luke's cruel revelations with a white face and burning eyes, breaking down only once, when he had told her about the coming baby. She had been stunned and reached for him disbelievingly, sick with shock and pain, but he had not responded. And in the months that followed she had put on as brave a face as she could, finishing her time at university, refusing to give in to the cowardly temptation not to go home for the holidays, prattling with mock sophistication to her friends about the life she was leading...the men she was dating...

Her parents had seen through her, though...and, aware of her anguish and, she suspected, of the deep wound Luke had dealt to the very essence of her womanhood, had announced that her father was taking semi-retirement and that they were all moving back to York, which had been her father's childhood home.

It had been a measure of the depth of the love she had once felt for Luke that she had almost refused to go with them...hoping against hope for the miracle that would give Luke back to her, unable to believe even now that it was really over. And then she had seen him in the village, with his wife and their child... He had been holding the baby, while his wife was talking earnestly to another couple. She had stopped dead in the street, measuring the distance between them and ignominiously preparing for flight. The baby had had dark hair like Luke's... A little girl, so Louise had told her apologetically, with embarrassment and compassion... And the girl who was his wife...younger than Jenneth, dark-haired, well-dressed and almost shy, she had looked at Jenneth, obviously not realising who she was, and had then turned to Luke, saying quite clearly as she took the baby from him, 'Come along, darling—I think it's time we left.'

Sick at heart, Jenneth hadn't gone home, but had gone instead down the path along the river, a favourite haunt from her early teens where she used to idle her way home from school after she'd left

Louise, daydreaming about life and Luke with all the innocence of her extreme youth.

Now, with a cynicism that sat oddly on her slender shoulders, she wondered what would have happened if she too had conceived Luke's child. And it had been a distinct possibility: right up to the very weekend before he had announced that he was ending their engagement and why, Luke had been trying to persuade her to allow them to become lovers.

She closed her eyes abruptly, not wanting to remember the fiercely impassioned way he had made love to her that summer, breaking off when she had pleaded with him to stop, as she tremulously explained that he would be her first lover, and that she was afraid.

He had seemed to understand, teasing her about her fears, but she had thought that underneath his amusement he had been pleased that he would be her first lover.

How often during those first arid months without him had she asked herself if things would have been different had *she* been different? But she had stalwartly refused to allow herself to believe that, if Luke had really loved her, he would have turned to someone else for the sexual satisfaction she had not given him.

His betrayal of her, though, had had a lasting effect on her awareness of herself as a woman, destroying something so intrinsic within her that, as the years passed, she had privately likened herself to an animated doll without any real deep inner core...love, desire, all the emotions which filled the lives of other people were a foreign territory to her. She loved the twins, of course, and she enjoyed the company of her few good friends, but in a one-to-one relationship with a man she discovered that she just could not function... The mere hint of anything approaching intimacy made her remember how she had suffered through Luke's rejection, and as the years passed she had deemed it wiser to hold the male sex well at bay. And now Louise was getting married... her friend who had always been so fiercely independent.

She knew that most people who knew her put her single state down to the responsibility she felt for the twins. It was a convenient excuse, but one she would no longer have once they were at university. Not that men were exactly beating a path to her door, urgently exclaiming their desire... She grimaced a little at the thought, mentally reviewing the men who had invited her out recently. There was Colin Ames, the local vet, a kind-hearted, rawboned man, divorced with three small children, who was quite obviously looking for a substitute mother not just for his children, she suspected, but for himself as well.

There was Greg Pilling, who at thirty-five was still single, and considered something of a heartbreaker locally; he had a large house on the other side of the village and business interests which took him to London for four days out of every seven. Privately Jenneth suspected he was involved with someone down there whose identity he wished to keep secret for reasons best known to himself... because she was already married? Jenneth wondered cynically.

There were one or two others, pleasant, kind men who were quite obviously excellent husband and father material, but she refused to allow herself to get involved.

It wasn't so much what Luke had done, she told herself these days, it was the fact that he had had the power to do it that made her avoid emotional commitments . . . it was the memory of her own intense vulnerability that kept her from allowing anyone too close to her.

Of course, in the years immediately following her parents' deaths, any kind of intimate relationship with a man had been impossible. The twins had needed her too much, and her life had been so closely tied up with theirs that there was no space in it for anyone else. But now the twins were virtually adult—and it was Louise who had unwillingly forced her into this introspective mood, Jenneth reflected wryly, standing up and acknowledging that it was impossible now to try and concentrate on her work.

It was too late now to wish she had not made the commitment to attend the wedding, even if Luke was not going to be there . . . there would be other people there who would remember . . .

What? That she and Luke had been engaged, eight years ago, for the space of less than six months? That that engagement had been broken and that Luke had married someone else, and that subsequently they had had a child? So what? It was only in her own mind that the spectre of Luke's rejection loomed so destructively . . .

Sometimes she suspected that Louise saw more than she said, even though her friend had accepted her explanations at face-value when she'd come home to discover that the engagement was over and that Luke was married to someone else.

It had been Louise who had given her the news some years ago that Luke's wife was dead...a postscript added to a birthday card that had shocked her into a week of nightmare dreams of such intense reality that she had woken from them sweating and crying, shivering under the burden of knowing that even now Luke had the power to affect her intensely both emotionally and physically.

That had been the year Louise had coaxed her to go home with her for Christmas, and because the twins had pleaded with her to accept the invitation she had given way, never expecting to find that Luke was also at home, visiting his aunt and uncle.

His father lived in America now, and Luke, who had followed his father into medicine, was a consultant at one of the large teaching hospitals.

The sight of him, so familiar and once so desperately dear, had frozen her to the floor of Louise's parents' hallway. The twins, walking in behind her, had bumped into her... Someone had made the necessary introductions, she couldn't remember who, and under cover of the general noise and confusion she had found herself confronting Luke, while her insides cringed with remembered anguish and misery, and she masked her face with the cool, remote smile she had perfected.

He had had his daughter with him, a bright, mischievous three-year-old, who plainly adored her daddy, and looked so like him that Jenneth had felt as though someone had slid a knife into her heart and turned it.

For some unfathomable reason she still didn't understand, and which had seemed unreasoningly cruel of fate, Luke's daughter had chosen to attach herself both to Jenneth and the twins, following them everywhere, watching them with Luke's dark green eyes, smiling at them with Luke's smile, but Jenneth had resisted the aching, yearning need within her to respond to the child's overtures, to pick her up and cuddle her, to open her arms to her and hold her as she so plainly wanted to be held, with something approaching Luke's proud, contemptuous disdain of her.

She remembered how Luke had walked into the sitting-room one day while she was there alone with Angelica, desperately trying to withstand the child's very obvious desire for feminine affection. He had picked his daughter up, plainly recognising both the withdrawal and rejection in Jenneth's refusal to touch his child, his mouth grim with dislike of her where once it had been soft with desire and love... or so she had thought. But that of course had just been an illusion.

She hadn't realised how he had interpreted the twins' adolescent teasing about the fact that she had very recently ended a brief relationship with one of her clients; nor that he had assumed quite wrongly from her brothers' totally erroneous description of that relationship that she and Christopher Harding had been lovers, but the barbed comment he had made to her about the dullness of his aunt and uncle's home without the presence of her lover to enliven it for her had been something she had seized gladly upon to bolster her shaky pride, smiling insincerely back at him as she said lightly, 'It's only for a week...'

And Luke had responded jeeringly, 'And you can live quite easily without him in your bed for that length of time, is that it?'

And then, with a rush of anger she could only regret later, she had retaliated rashly—and thoroughly untruthfully—saying, 'Christopher and I have been lovers for quite some time,' and then from somewhere she had produced a feline smile, and added, 'He goes away on business quite a lot, and when he does...'

'You replace him in your bed with someone else,' Luke had finished for her, totally misunderstanding what she had been about to say, which was that when Christopher was away she coped quite adequately without him. Before she could correct him, he had continued bitterly, 'How you've changed. And to think that——'

He had stopped speaking as the twins came bursting into the room, and after that they had each studiously avoided the other, Luke taking good care to make sure his small daughter came nowhere near her.

She had told herself that she had been glad...glad that she had finally shown him that she was a woman and desirable to others, even if not to him...glad that she had made it clear that she wanted nothing to do with him or with his child...glad that she had finally and irrevocably broken away from the old Jenneth, who had adored him to the point of lunacy, who had loved him just as intensely...and who had gone on loving him long after he had made it plain that he most certainly did not love her.

And that had been the last time she had seen him.

CHAPTER TWO

As THE date of Louise's wedding drew closer, Jenneth found herself regretting more and more that she had agreed to go. It was not that she didn't *want* to see her friend married and wish her and her new husband good luck; she did, and, had Louise chosen anywhere but Little Compton as the venue for her wedding, Jenneth knew that she would have been anticipating it with a glad heart, and more than a touch of delighted curiosity about the man who had so radically changed her old friend's determined stance on the joys of the single state.

As it was, even with Louise's reassurance that Luke would not be attending the wedding, she was increasingly conscious of the fact that there would be other people there who remembered her younger self, and her love for Luke; they would remember their engagement and Luke's subsequent marriage to someone else; and then, in the manner of village people the world over, they would look at her ringless hands and speculate among themselves as to the reasons for her unmarried state.

Standing in her studio, she gave a tiny shudder of revulsion at the thought of their curiosity and pity, wishing that she had the courage to telephone Louise and tell her firmly that she could not attend the wedding. There were, after all, half a dozen genuine reasons she could conjure up for not attending, and one of them was in front of her now on her desk, she acknowledged ruefully, frowning over the preliminary sketches she had been asked to prepare for a large mural to cover the walls of the children's ward in one of York's large hospitals.

The commission had come to her via a client of hers, who had spearheaded a campaign to raise funds to support the specialised ward, which had been in danger of collapsing.

An exceedingly large donation from a millionaire local businessman had resulted not only in the ward being fully re-equipped with several vital pieces of advanced technology, but there had also been sufficient money left over for her ex-client, who was chairwoman of the fund-raising committee, to announce briskly that they could afford to do something about the almost institutionalised drabness of the ward's emulsion-painted walls.

She had approached Jenneth, who had been delighted to accept the commission, which she had offered to do at much less than her normal rates, and in return she had virtually been given *carte blanche* with the design.

The problem now facing her was what to choose to catch the imagination and attention of children suffering so desperately, and of such very disparate ages.

Her lack of concentration in favour of worrying about the ordeal of Louise's wedding didn't help, and she was still frowning over the vague notes she had scribbled down when the studio door opened and Kit came in.

Jenneth watched him walking towards her with the familiar loping stride that both he and his twin had inherited from their father, her heart as always caught up in a wave of mingled love and apprehension... Love because they were both so very dear to her, and apprehension because guiding two exuberant and very high-spirited boys through their teenage years had not always been easy.

Their A levels now behind them, and the long summer holiday just begun, Jenneth realised anew with almost every day that passed that they were now virtually adult. Certainly both of them were emotionally mature and well-balanced, something for which she modestly refused to take the credit, putting it down to the fact that their parents had provided them all with a stable and loving background during their early years.

Kit grinned at her as he advanced towards her and asked, 'Any chance of borrowing your car? I'm playing tennis over at Chris Harding's this afternoon, and Nick's taken the Metro.'

The rather battered but roadworthy Metro that Jenneth had bought them as a joint eighteenth birthday present had done sterling service in the six months they had owned it, but, although they were twins, her brothers enjoyed different hobbies and had different sets of friends. So far she had ignored the broad hints she had been given about the necessity for another car. The hints had been good-humoured, both boys being well aware that, although their father's insurance policies had provided a roof over their heads, and a small but steady income, any luxuries had to be paid for out of Jenneth's commissions.

Since they were both sensible and very good drivers, she had no qualms about loaning them her

own car when she wasn't using it, but on this occasion she shook her head with genuine regret and
explained, 'I have to go in to York with some
paintings for the gallery, and I promised Eleanor
I'd do it this afternoon. I could drop you off on
the way, if you like,' she offered obligingly.

'Only if you let me drive,' Kit countered with a
grin. It was a standing joke between them that
Jenneth, inclined to daydream, especially when her
work engrossed her, was sometimes rather an er-
ratic driver. She blushed even now to recall the occasion on which she had been so deeply involved
mentally in the mural she was working on that she
had driven down the narrow lane that led from their
house to the main road and straight into a ditch,
necessitating an anxious call to their nearest
neighbour, a local farmer, who obligingly came out
with his tractor to haul her sturdy Volvo estate car
back on to the lane.

Kit and Nick knew all about Louise's forth-
coming wedding and, although she hadn't said so
to them, both of them were also aware of Jenneth's
reluctance to attend, just as they were both also
fully aware of her inner withdrawal whenever the
subject of Little Compton and its inhabitants came
up.

Both of them were far too fond and protective
of their sister to probe, but both of them were also
curious. Although Jenneth herself was unaware of
it, they had taken on bets on whether or not she
would attend the wedding, and Kit, who had bet
his twin that she would, intended to make use of
the drive to his friend's house to ensure that she
did.

Not very long ago he and Nick had put their heads together, and decided that before they left for university they would have to do something about their sister's future.

'She needs to get married,' Kit had announced, causing Nick to lift his eyebrows and jeer 'chauvinist' at him. But Kit had shaken his head, and replied, 'I don't mean it that way... Sure, financially she can support herself—after all, she's supported us for long enough—but don't you sometimes think that it's almost as though there's a part of her missing somehow? She needs a husband and a family.'

'To take her mind off what we're getting up to?' Nick suggested with a grin.

Although physically identical, emotionally they were very different, but on this occasion both of them had agreed that they had somehow or other to sort out their sister's life for her, so that when they left she would not be on her own.

To this end they had conducted an exhaustive survey to find a man they considered suitable to become Jenneth's husband, and their brother-in-law.

Their hopes had risen to a high-water mark after the incident of Jenneth's accidental journey into the ditch; Tim Soames was virtually their next-door neighbour, single, comfortably off, the right age—a pleasant, easygoing man, with broad shoulders and a ruddy face.

He obligingly assisted them by asking Jenneth out, but after a couple of dates and several visits to the house he had suddenly stopped calling and, when pressed, Jenneth had told them calmly that although she liked him she didn't want to get involved.

That was the whole trouble, Kit reflected, darting a quick glance at his sister as she slid into the passenger seat beside him. She didn't want to get involved. But she needed someone in her life…someone who would care for her and protect her. Someone who would see beneath the calm surface to the real person below.

They had the car windows open because of the heat; the countryside was in a rare spate of perfect June weather, and the draught caught at her hair, tangling its silky smoothness. Jenneth lifted her hand to push it out of the way, reflecting irritably that she really ought to have it cut and that shoulder-length hair on a woman of twenty-nine was an absurd and foolish clinging to a youth long gone.

Watching her, Kit grinned to himself, remembering a jealous girlfriend of Nick's who had bitterly refused to believe that Jenneth was their sister, having seen her and Nick out together, and been convinced that Nick was two-timing her; and it was true that no one who didn't know them would ever guess that there was over ten years between them.

'I suppose while you're in York you'll be looking for an outfit to wear for Louise's wedding,' announced Kit, with male superiority for the female of the species' preoccupation with clothes, something which must surely be instilled in the male psyche at conception, Jenneth reflected crossly, because he certainly hadn't learned that male disparagement of her sex's vanities from her.

She took the bait as Kit had known she would, reminding him sardonically that it had been less than four months ago that he had virtually retired to his bedroom in a sulk, and all because Nick had borrowed his treasured original 501s. She was totally unaware of the fact that she was already the victim of the opening salvo in Kit's battle to win his bet.

After she had dropped him off at his friend's house, Jenneth continued her journey to York, wryly admitting that clothes for the wedding had been the last thing on her mind, and equally acknowledging that it would be perceived by the other guests as an insult to Louise if she did not turn up dressed accordingly.

Eleanor Coombes, her partner in the gallery, a brisk, cheerful widow in her mid-forties with a married daughter and one small granddaughter, welcomed her warmly when she parked her car at the rear of their small premises just inside the city wall.

It didn't take them long to unload the canvases; in addition to Jenneth's own work they sold work by other local artists, mainly watercolour landscapes, and offered a framing and restoration service, which was Eleanor's contribution to the business.

Eleanor came from a wealthy background; she had met her husband while in Italy on a post-university course in the restoration of paintings, skills which she had not used during her marriage. However, after her husband's death, finding herself virtually alone in the huge, gaunt house twenty miles outside York, her daughter working away in

London and time hanging heavily on her hands, she had been introduced to Jenneth at a party given by a mutual acquaintance. Their friendship had grown, and ultimately Eleanor had approached Jenneth with an offer to finance a gallery in partnership with Jenneth, suggesting that she should take care of the day-to-day running of the business, leaving Jenneth free to spend more time painting. She also acted in part as Jenneth's unofficial agent, and since their partnership had begun Jenneth acknowledged that her commissions had almost doubled.

'Something wrong?' Eleanor asked her, noticing her absorbed manner and slight frown.

Jenneth shook her head. 'Not really... An old friend—my best friend, actually—is getting married next weekend, and she wants me to go to the wedding...'

'And you haven't a thing to wear,' guessed Eleanor with a grin, tactfully not commenting on the wary shadow that darkened her friend's eyes. She had learned over the years to allow Jenneth her privacy, but she, like the twins, although with a good deal more experience of life and far more maturity, often reflected that it was an appalling waste that a young woman so obviously designed by nature to nurture and mother should have so firmly turned her back on any relationship that would have allowed her to fulfil that role.

Eleanor was no misty-eyed romantic. Her own marriage had not been easy; her husband had been almost twenty years her senior and very demanding, but they had loved one another and had gradually come to understand how to make allow-

ances for one another's needs and prejudices. She
genuinely missed his companionship and mourned
his death, even though she had been a widow for
over seven years. Unlike Jenneth, though, her life
wasn't devoid of an emotional and sexual relationship. She had a lover: a divorced man whose relationship with his wife had left him wary and
bitter; she was wise enough and mature enough to
accept the pleasure and happiness that the relationship gave her, without needing or wanting more
than John was able to give. She had reached an age
where she prized her own independence... which
she had no intention of relinquishing in order to
take on the potential problems of a second marriage to a man with two very possessive and sometimes aggressive teenage daughters, and a whole
host of emotional problems of his own that could
not be solved by the pleasure they gave one another
in bed.

Jenneth's case was different, though. Jenneth was
born to be a mother... and if the more feminist of
her peers felt it necessary to take her to task for
such a view, then let them. There was nothing
wrong in being a woman who was emotionally designed first and foremost to fulfil that role, and it
was her view that by suppressing it, Jenneth was
destroying an intrinsic part of herself. She whole-
heartedly shared the twins' view that Jenneth should
marry.

'Mmm... well, there's no shortage of excellent
dress shops in York,' she said now, ignoring the
way Jenneth's body tightened as though she was
mentally preparing for flight. From what? Eleanor
wondered curiously, studying her friend while ap-

pearing not to do so. 'I could come with you, if you like,' she offered. 'Rachel's coming in this afternoon—I was going to spend a couple of hours doing the books...'

Jenneth knew when she was being backed into a corner. And, realistically, she could hardly not go to the wedding. Louise would be hurt, and since Luke was not going to be there... Not for the first time, Jenneth wished that fate had seen fit to bestow upon her a nature that was less vulnerable.

'Petrol tank's full, tyres and oil are checked... Your suitcase is in the back...'

Jenneth raised her eyes heavenwards as Nick calmly ticked these items off on his fingers. Anyone listening would have thought that she was the twins' junior and not the other way around. She wasn't travelling south in the outfit Eleanor had bullied her into buying for the wedding. Instead she had allowed herself sufficient time to go to the Feathers beforehand and get changed.

It was barely seven o'clock on a Saturday morning, the sky a soft blue, hazed over with a mist that promised heat for later in the day. A perfect late June day...

In Little Compton, Louise, who had decided to spend several days at home before the wedding, would probably just be waking up. She had confessed to Jenneth over the telephone that she had succumbed to persuasion and temptation and had bought herself a wedding dress that bid to outshine anything that Scarlett O'Hara might ever have worn...

'Cream and not white,' Louise had told her, with her rich, unabashed chuckle.

George was far from being the first man in her friend's life; Louise wasn't promiscuous, but there had been several men with whom she had fallen in love, several lovers in her life from whom she had always managed to part on good terms, and it was obvious from what she had said to Jenneth that neither she nor George regretted those previous relationships.

It was going to be a long drive south, and Jenneth had decided to ignore the motorways because of the number of roadworks causing major delays.

By the twins' reckoning she would reach Little Compton by twelve o'clock at the latest. Louise was getting married at three, and she had promised to be at the house to help her friend get ready beforehand and then afterwards to help her get changed before she and George left for their honeymoon.

'A kind of unofficial bridesmaid,' Louise had told her, and Jenneth had winced, remembering how once she had eagerly made Louise promise to perform that office for her.

The drive south was without incident, the roads, although busy, not oppressively so.

She reached the familiar countryside east of Bath just before eleven o'clock. Outwardly very little had changed in the seven years since she had left, although the large number of German marque cars bore witness to the fact that the new motorway was making this part of the country more accessible to those who earned their living in London.

Little Compton itself was just far away enough from the motorway to be unaffected by these changes. As she crested one of the gentle hills that surrounded it, Jenneth slowed down to look down on the untidy straggle of cottages that marked its one main road, the Feathers at one end of it, and the church at the other.

She suppressed the memories that threatened to come storming back . . . long, lazy summer afternoons spent with Luke, the young Jenneth bemused and thrilled by the almost magical way he had suddenly realised that she was no longer just a friend of his cousin's but a person in her own right. Down there where the river meandered its lazy course, a glistening, fluid ribbon shadowed by willows, Luke had kissed her for the first time. Without wanting to, Jenneth remembered how her whole body had responded to that kiss, almost vibrating with shocked pleasure like a highly tuned instrument. He had laughed tenderly against her mouth and asked her if she knew what it did to him to feel that kind of response. It had been in that same spot only three months later that he had proposed to her, saying tersely that he knew he was rushing her, but that he was leaving to work in California at the end of the summer and that he wanted to take with him her promise to wait for him.

Later, when she had given him her breathless, almost incredulous answer, he had taken her in his arms and kissed her with a fierce passion that had set her heart pounding and made her totally unable to resist when he had laid her down on the soft grass beneath the trees and, between kisses that turned her bones to liquid, gently unfastened the shirt she was wearing to bare her breasts first to his eyes, then to his hands and, finally, shockingly and blissfully, to his mouth.

If he had pressed her then, they would have been lovers, but he hadn't and, once the announcement of their engagement had been made, their time alone together had seemed to diminish, mainly because Luke's mother's health had started to deteriorate, and Jenneth had fully understood and backed his need to put his mother first.

Shaking her head to dispel the unwanted images shimmering just below the surface of her mind, she put her foot on the accelerator and turned firmly away, driving towards the village.

The landlady of the Feathers welcomed her warmly, and showed her immediately to her room, a comfortably furnished attic with a dormer window, and its own private bathroom... The Feathers had once, long ago in the days of coach travel, been a posting house, and Jenneth's bedroom overlooked the enclosed courtyard to the rear of the village street.

'Louise said you'd prefer to be in here,' the landlady told her cheerfully, and as Jenneth agreed with her calm, slightly remote smile she reflected that it was typical of Louise that she should be known to everyone in the village by her Christian name, even though her visits home were these days limited to flying half-day stays at Christmas and other anniversaries.

The Feathers had changed hands since Jenneth's day, and the landlady was more interested in talking about the wedding and the amazement it had caused in the village than displaying curiosity about Jenneth herself. Her indifference released some of Jenneth's tension, and as the landlady left, promising to send someone up with a light salad lunch and a pot of coffee, Jenneth reflected ruefully that she had probably blown people's reaction to her appearance at the wedding totally out of proportion. This realisation helped to steady her nerves, and when a shy waitress came upstairs with the promised lunch Jenneth felt relaxed enough to pick up the telephone and dial the familiar number of Louise's family home.

Louise's mother answered the telephone, recognising Jenneth's voice immediately and responding warmly to her hesitant enquiries as to the state of the bride-to-be.

By the time Louise herself picked up the receiver, she was ready to dismiss all her fears as simply the working of her own self-indulgent imagination, and agreed readily to go straight round to the house immediately she had changed.

She chose not to drive her car to Louise's parents' home, but to walk there instead, not down the main street of the village, but along the path that ran behind the cottages and then skirted the churchyard.

Jenneth had always found it slightly surprising that her outspoken, very modern-minded friend should be the daughter of a vicar, and she knew that, to David Simmonds' credit, he had never tried to impose his own religious beliefs on his daughter.

He greeted Jenneth warmly as, through habit, she walked round to the back door of the vicarage and he opened it to her knock. Louise's mother bustled into the kitchen and kissed Jenneth affectionately. A tall, dark-haired woman, she betrayed her physical relationship to Luke's father and to Luke himself, having the same strong bone-structure and thick, dark hair. Louise, she had always insisted, was a throw-back, and certainly her friend's vivid red hair and pale, creamy skin bore no resemblance to either of her parents' colouring.

Jenneth was told to go straight upstairs, and found her friend sitting in front of her bedroom mirror, clad in an almost indecently feminine chemise of cream satin and lace while she peered myopically into the mirror and tried to apply mascara to her lashes.

'Damn!' she exploded as Jenneth walked in.

'Let me do it for you,' suggested Jenneth calmly, taking charge and deftly applying the necessary coats of dark grey colour to the long but sandy lashes, asking humorously, 'What happened to the contact lenses?'

'I daren't risk them,' Louise replied gloomily. 'I'm bound to start howling and wash the damn things out . . .'

'There's always your glasses,' Jenneth told her mischievously.

As a schoolgirl Louise had been obliged to wear the regulation National Health corrective glasses, and now she scowled horribly into Jenneth's laughing eyes and threatened, 'You dare mention those . . .'

The scowl disappeared as they both burst out laughing and, ignoring her perfection of her deli-cately made-up face and the artfully arranged tumble of red curls that brushed her naked shoulders, Louise stood up and hugged Jenneth af-

fectionately, saying emotionally, 'Oh, Jen, I'm so
glad you're here...'

Listening to her, Jenneth felt guilty and ashamed
of her craven impulse to renege on her promise,
and hugged her back in a silent exchange of emotion
that held memories of the years and times they had
shared.

'Isn't this ridiculous?' Louise sniffed as Jenneth
released her. 'I feel as weepy and emotional as a
Jane Austen heroine...'

'You certainly aren't dressed like one,' Jenneth
told her forthrightly, eyeing the extremely provocative creation of satin and lace that purported to have
the utilitarian purpose of sleeking her friend's soft
curves and supporting the delicate cream stockings
she was wearing.

Louise grinned at her, totally unabashed.

'Like it? George chose it,' she told Jenneth
wickedly, and then drew her attention to the tiny
row of satin-covered buttons that fastened down
the front.

'He said that thinking about me wearing this is
the only thing that's going to keep him going
through the whole ordeal of the ceremony,' she
added with another grin, and Jenneth was forced
to mentally review her opinion of her friend's
husband-to-be. Despite his name, he was obviously
far from being the stalwart, sober, almost dull
character she had envisaged.

From downstairs, they both heard Louise's
mother call up warningly, 'You've only got half an
hour left, Louise...' and, remembering her supposed role, Jenneth picked up the billowing silk and
net underskirt from the bed and presented it to her

friend, helping her to fasten the tapes that tied at the back, and then helping her into the frothing creation of raw silk and lace that had swung gently in the breeze from the window.

Stupidly, once the last small button had been fastened, and she was able to walk in front of her friend and survey the finished effect, Jenneth discovered that her eyes were misty with tears and her voice choked with emotion.

'You look... wonderful...' was all she could manage, but it seemed to be enough, because Louise hugged her tightly and then swore huskily.

'Damn! I daren't start wailing now or my blessed mascara is bound to run...' And then, more soberly, she said, 'Jen, this should be you and not me. You're made for marriage... children...' A frown touched her face and, sensing instinctively that she was about to mention Luke, Jenneth trembled with relief when the door suddenly opened and Louise's parents came in with a bottle of champagne and four glasses.

By the time they had toasted the bride and allowed her one glass of champagne to bolster her failing courage, it was time to leave for the church.

Louise had elected to walk there, proudly escorted by her father, and it seemed to Jenneth, watching her from the sidelines, that the whole village had turned out to wish her well.

Louise's godfather was giving her away, and Jenneth felt tears spring to her eyes as her father handed her over to his cousin before disappearing inside the church where he would conduct the ceremony.

Most of the guests were already inside, and Jenneth hurried to her own place in a pew to the rear of the small, quiet building, just in time to watch Louise drift beautifully down the aisle.

Although she tried not to let it do so, the familiarity of the comfortable church where she herself had once envisaged being married made her ache inside with a pain she had thought she was long ago past feeling.

Her eyes blurred with tears which she readily recognised were not for the awe and mysticism of the service, but, self-pityingly, for herself. Through the blur of them she was distantly aware of someone entering the pew: a young girl with dark, shiny hair, framing an elfin face, and dressed in a pretty, crisp cotton dress, with a dropped waistline and a neat sailor collar. Behind the girl was a man, but Jenneth didn't look at him, all her concentration fixed on the bride and groom as she willed herself not to give in to the tears burning the backs of her eyes and making her throat raw with pain.

It was stupidity and self-indulgent folly to remember that once she had believed that *she* would be married here . . . that *she* would walk down the narrow ancient aisle to find Luke waiting for her . . . to have their marriage blessed and sanctified here in the mellow darkness of the church where members of his family had been married for so many generations.

Some memories, though, could not be suppressed . . . like the one of Luke bringing her in here when he'd given her her engagement ring, and kissing her finger before sliding on to it the narrow band of gold with its brilliant ring of diamond fire surrounding the central sapphire. He had kissed her once, tenderly, chastely... her mouth twisted over her almost medieval choice of word, and yet there was nothing else that truly described the sanctity of that moment... and her body shook, racked by a tremor of anguish as she fought to suppress the memories threatening to overwhelm her and acknowledged inwardly that this had been what she had feared. Not the speculative looks of others, but her own deep inner vulnerability... her own painful memories... her own still aching need to understand just what had motivated Luke to deceive her so cruelly and surely so unnecessarily. Why get engaged to her in the first place if he had known all along that all he wanted from her was a sexual relationship? Why make promises he had no intention of keeping when he must have known she was so fathoms deep in love with him that she would have given herself to him blindly, with the right kind of persuasion?

The tears she was fighting to suppress overwhelmed her, and ran betrayingly down her face. She bent her head protectively, hoping the soft swing of her hair would conceal her face from the other people in the pew beside her, and bit her bottom lip hard to suppress the vast welling of emotion that threatened her. And then, to her astonishment, she felt something soft touch her hand, and a low but insistent little voice whispered urgently to her.

'You can use my handkerchief, if you like... I brought two because Daddy said that ladies always need them at weddings...' This last statement was delivered importantly, as though everything that

Daddy said ought to be recorded in the statute books, and Jenneth turned her head automatically, unable to resist the confiding voice and gesture. The handkerchief was crumpled and colourful but, because all her life she had loved and understood children, Jenneth took it, and firmly blew her nose on it while she and her rescuer exchanged conspiratorial feminine glances.

'I wanted to bring some confetti,' her new friend confided engagingly, obviously deciding that the loan of the handkerchief and its acceptance constituted a basis for shared confidences. 'But Mrs. Mack wouldn't buy any for me. She doesn't approve of weddings.'

In front of them the bridal pair were making their vows. Louise's father gave the blessing and above them the organ music swelled triumphantly; as though on cue, the church doors were flung open to admit the brilliance of the June sunshine, and high up in the church tower the great bells which had been cast in the same year that St Paul's rose from its ashes gave joyful tongue to the happiness of the hour.

Automatically, as the light flooded the church behind them, Jenneth turned her head, and then froze with shock as she found herself looking straight into the familiar features of the one person she would have fled to the ends of the earth to avoid.

'Luke...'

His name was a strangled sound on her lips, the shocked pallor of her face causing the man watching her to narrow his eyes consideringly as he looked from her blonde head to his daughter's dark one.

It had been a last-minute decision to attend his cousin's wedding, prompted by his daughter's very obvious but patiently borne disappointment, rather than any desire to see Louise married.

If the news of his appointment had not meant the cancellation of his lecture tour in America less than a week after it had begun he wouldn't have been here at all. Angelica had expressed herself delighted to learn that she was going to have her father's company during the long school holidays after all, and had been even more pleased to learn that they would be moving from London to a city called York, which her father had told her she would like very much.

Since she readily accepted her father's word as being above and beyond that of any other authority, she was envisaging the impending move with a pleasure and excitement that was only in part tinged with the knowledge that their existing housekeeper, with whom she was not always in accord, would not be moving with them.

Angelica didn't enjoy being the responsibility of a housekeeper. What she wanted was a real mother like other girls had . . . but to achieve that her father would have to remarry, and she had judiciously over the last few months been casting her eye about in order to supply the need in their lives that her father seemed neglectful in attending to . . .

For a moment Jenneth actually thought she was going to faint, but then pride came to her rescue, and she forced herself to regain control of her failing senses, wondering bitterly what premeditated cruelty it was that had motivated Luke to choose this particular pew, and to curse her own susceptibility in believing Louise's assurances that her cousin was not going to attend the wedding.

The bride and groom were coming down the aisle towards them. Angelica, blissfully unaware of the fierce undercurrents seething between the two adults, grasped Jenneth's hand and demanded, 'Doesn't she look lovely?' Then, without realising it, she acquitted Louise of any blame for Luke's appearance by adding innocently, 'We weren't going to come today, but Daddy had to come back from America because he's got a new job, and I persuaded him to bring me...' This was accompanied by a wide beam of pleasure, to which Jenneth in her vulnerable and defenceless state found it impossible not to respond.

'Can we sit with you at the reception?' Angelica asked eagerly, following up her advantage with innocent swiftness. 'I don't have a mummy and I don't like the way people look at me and Daddy when we're on our own,' she confided appealingly to Jenneth, while in the background Jenneth heard Luke snap warningly,

'Angelica, that's enough...'

As tears started in the clear green eyes, so like Luke's that Jenneth acknowledged she ought to have known immediately who she was, she found herself instinctively protecting the child from her father's anger, saying fiercely, 'Don't...' and then, before she could overcome her own shock, Angelica announced happily,

'See, Daddy, she doesn't mind at all. I knew you wouldn't... 'Cos you're here on your own, too, aren't you?' she said artlessly, adding with a childish forthrightness that struck Jenneth to the heart, 'You aren't wearing a wedding ring, so that means that you're not married, doesn't it? And I expect you don't want to sit on your own either. It will be fun,' she finished, beaming up at Jenneth. 'We can pretend that we're a real family...'

And, before Jenneth could make the appalled denial that was choking in her throat, Louise and George drew level with them, and she had a moment's startled realisation that her friend's husband looked nothing like George-like, and that Louise was wearing a totally unfamiliar look of blissful bemusement that made her own heart ache treacherously.

Somehow or other she discovered that she was outside with the rest of the guests crowding around the newly married couple, and that Angelica had fixed herself firmly to her side, and was clutching her hand with what almost amounted to possessiveness, chattering brightly to her so that Jenneth hadn't the heart to reject her and quell the happiness in her eyes by telling her that she wanted nothing to do with her.

It was several moments before they managed to break through the crush to reach Louise, and when her friend saw the little girl clinging firmly to Jenneth's side, her eyes darkened with dismay and she said uncertainly, 'Jenneth, I promise you I had no idea...'

Before Jenneth could say anything, Angelica clutched even harder at her hand and announced, not just to Louise, but also to the crowd of people within earshot of her carrying, piping voice, 'Jenneth's going to be my pretend mummy, Aunt Louise.'

As Jenneth heard the hard male voice say warningly behind her, 'Angelica,' she felt the shock of her body's awareness of Luke's tall male presence behind her, and her body trembled so visibly that she was not surprised to see the concern in Louise's eyes.

If she had felt that the day could hold nothing worse than it had already held, she found she was wrong, when she heard Louise's mother saying firmly. 'Luke, Jenneth looks as though she's about to faint . . . help her, will you?'

Against her back and arm she felt the hands whose touch had tormented her dreams for far too many years, holding her firmly but dispassionately, as Luke briskly obeyed his aunt's instructions and manoeuvred her out of the crush of people around the church porch and into the privacy of the churchyard.

Now, when she would have given anything to faint and thereby escape a situation which was fast outstripping the very worst of her nightmares, her body remained stubbornly determined not to allow her that escape.

Instinctively she pulled away from Luke, not surprised that he let her go—he must be loathing this every bit as much as she was, but he could only be suffering revulsion, and not the agonising awareness of feelings she ached to be able to deny which were oppressing her.

'How are you getting back to the house?' she heard him asking her distantly, and, too surprised to lie, she told him.

'Walking? In this heat?' She watched the dark eyebrows draw together, and saw that the years had not been entirely kind to him and that, although nothing ever could diminish his masculinity, there were hard grooves etched either side of his mouth, and tiny lines fanning out from his eyes, suggesting that his life had not been without pain.

That should have made her feel glad, but it didn't. She had an appalling, impossible impulse to reach out and touch him. To smooth those lines away...to make him smile, the old, familiar, teasing smile that had once made her stomach curl with pleasure and her body ache with desire.

'My car's just round the corner. We'll give you a lift...'

'No!' The panic-stricken denial was out before she could stop it, leaving them both to look at one another in a silence that was impregnated with an emotional hostility Jenneth could almost taste.

In the distance the photographer was busily at work, and she could hear the hum of conversation, but it was a distant, unobtrusive hum, as though she and Luke were sealed into an intimacy that locked out the rest of the human race.

And then Angelica piped up shrilly and uncertainly, 'But, Jenneth, you promised that you were going to be my pretend mummy...'

Under the sardonic, bitter eyes of her father Jenneth turned towards the little girl, the words of denial burning her throat until she saw the vulnerable look in her eyes and knew that she just could not do it.

CHAPTER THREE

THE rest of the afternoon turned into a nightmare over which Jenneth felt she had no control whatsoever. Angelica had attached herself to her with all the skill and determination of a limpet. Although in other circumstances she might have been able to detach herself sufficiently to feel a certain degree of unkind amusement at Luke's very obvious frustration with his daughter's apparent instant rapport with her, at the moment, all her energy was concentrated on simply getting through the appalling ordeal without betraying to anyone just what she was going through. She was only too aware of the curious, knowing eyes on her of people who had watched her grow up and fall in love with the man now seated opposite her at one of the beautifully decorated round tables in the marquee on the vicarage lawn.

It wasn't just the shock of Luke's unexpected arrival... it wasn't just her sharp wariness of the interest and speculation they were causing. No, what she was feeling went deeper than that, and hurt so painfully that even drawing breath made her throat ache... What she was experiencing was an intense bitter-sweet awareness of how easy it would be to let time slip back, and to pretend, as Angelica was so happily doing, that the three of them belonged together... that they *were* the family unit Angelica had confided to her she wanted so much; and it was this awareness of the extent of her vulnerability that threatened her even more than Luke's presence.

When, after barely touching the delicious buffet, he excused himself, saying that he must go and make his peace with his aunt and uncle for his late arrival, Jenneth expelled a shaky breath of relief. Her stomach was tied in knots and her throat ached with tension. Angelica, who had demurely refused to go with him, smiled warmly at her and eyed her thoughtfully. Luke returned for the speeches and toasts, and as soon as they were over it was Jenneth's turn to excuse herself, saying quite truthfully that she had promised to help Louise get changed.

Angelica wanted to go with her, but Luke restrained her, and it was only as she got shakily to her feet to walk away from him that Jenneth realised that they had barely exchanged more than half a dozen grimly polite words in all the time they had been together.

Her heart sank with the acknowledgement, knowing that Luke had found the embarrassment of them being thrown together equally as onerous as she had done herself.

She said as much to Louise when the two of them were alone in Louise's bedroom. It was at the side of the house, overlooking an old-fashioned rose garden, and the scent of the bourbon roses came wafting into the room from the open french windows.

Louise's bedroom had a tiny wrought-iron balcony, with french windows opening on to it, and as teenagers they had both giggled over the possibility of some romantic Lothario climbing up the thorny roses outside to serenade Louise...

Listening to her impassioned outburst, Louise eyed her friend thoughtfully, and then said quietly, 'I think you're wrong, Jenneth. After all, if Luke hadn't wanted to sit with you, he needn't have...'

'Angelica didn't give him any choice in the matter,' Jenneth told her bitterly.

Louise chuckled. 'No, she does seem to have taken quite a fancy to you, doesn't she? Poor kid— I feel sorry for her, I must admit... Luke's away from home more than he's there, and his house-keeper, although very efficient, is scarcely warm-hearted...' She looked thoughtfully at her friend and added quietly, 'It's no secret in the family that Angelica would dearly love Luke to marry again. She told Ma last Christmas that all she really wanted was a proper mother. Poor Ma. She told me she was dumbfounded; Luke had bought the kid a bike...'

'Not a very good mother-substitute,' Jenneth agreed jerkily. She ached to tell her friend that she didn't want these confidences, that she wasn't strong enough to withstand them, and that the mere thought of Luke marrying again made her feel sick with the force of feelings she had thought long ago safely banished from her life.

One glance into his eyes... one second's realis-ation of his presence... that was all it had taken to show her that, whatever she had chosen to tell herself, nothing had changed. He still had the power to affect her on such a basic level that she was prac-tically in shock from the intensity of it.

She hadn't realised that Louise was looking at her, and, as their eyes met in the mirror and she saw the sympathy in her friend's, she jerked her head away... But Louise had known her too long and cared for her too much to remain silent.

'You still love him, don't you?' she said softly.

Jenneth gave a shudder and a tense, dry sob, shaking her head in a useless denial.

'Oh, Jen...I'm so sorry. I should have guessed. The way you refused to talk about your engagement to him... The way you've avoided him all these years...' Louise gnawed her bottom lip and said ruefully, 'Today must have been hell for you.'

Jenneth made a strangled sound in her throat. If what she had already gone through was hell, then this was purgatory itself. She loathed discussing her feelings with other people...even with someone as close to her as Louise.

'Which reminds me,' Louise added thoughtfully, ignoring her withdrawal. 'I meant to tax you with it before, but somehow or other it slipped my mind. Luke asked me the most peculiar question about you last Christmas...'

Jenneth who had been busy unfastening the buttons securing Louise's wedding dress, tensed, unable to believe that Luke felt enough curiosity about her to ask any questions, never mind peculiar ones.

'Let's go and stand by the window,' Louise suggested. 'The heat in here's stifling...'

Obligingly, Jenneth moved with her until they were standing right in front of the open balcony doors.

'No one will be able to see us,' she told Jenneth comfortably as she stepped out of her dress. 'Dad's banned everyone from going anywhere near his precious roses. Now, where was I? Last Christmas... Luke collared me while I was in the kitchen stacking the dishwasher, and made a derisive comment about the number and stamina of your legion of lovers, and said something about being curious to know whether you were ever likely to deign to marry any of them...'

When Jenneth made no response, she turned round and took hold of her friend's shoulders, forcing Jenneth to meet her eyes as she said quietly, 'Jen, you and I both know there hasn't been *one* lover, never mind an unending procession of them...'

There was a long, painful pause, and then Jenneth asked unsteadily, 'Did you tell Luke that?'

'No,' Louise assured her. 'But I must admit I was curious about where he'd got hold of such an erroneous impression of you.'

Another long pause, and then Jenneth said reluctantly, '*I* gave it to him. I...' Then, knowing that Louise wouldn't be satisfied until she had dragged the full story from her, she explained, 'It was that year we spent Christmas with you, and Luke turned up with Angelica. Mum and Dad hadn't been dead very long then, and I suppose I was feeling emotionally vulnerable. Seeing Luke with Angelica... and being reminded...' She bit her lip and then, when she had regained control of herself, said quietly, 'From something the twins said, Luke got the impression that I was having a physical relationship with a man who in actual fact was only a very casual friend. He taxed me with it, making several cutting remarks about how I'd changed...' She gave a tired shrug. 'I let him think he was right...and more... Out of pride, I suppose. I didn't want him to think I was still the same stupid child who had mooned about after him like an idiot...'

'Mmm... well, you certainly deceived him to good effect,' Louise told her drily. 'Odd, that... Luke's always been almost uncomfortably percipient. I should have thought he'd have seen right through that kind of pretence, especially when...'

'It's so obvious that I'm lacking in sexual allure,' Jenneth finished bitterly for her, but Louise ignored her acid tone and corrected mildly,

'What I was going to say was when the two of you had been so close.'

'"Had been" being the operative tense,' Jenneth reminded her. 'Anyway, it's all in the past and totally unimportant now...'

'If you discount the fact that you still love him,' Louise reminded her. 'Remember?'

Jenneth bit her lip, terrified that she was going to break down completely. 'Don't, please...' she managed in a stifled voice that brought a soft sound of regret to her friend's lips. And then Jenneth said fiercely, 'I *remember* all right, Louise. I *remember* how he came to me and told me that he was breaking off our engagement because another girl was having his child.'

Louise looked at her in compassionate sympathy and said ruefully, 'I'm so sorry, Jen... I *have* been blind, haven't I?'

She would have pursued the subject, but Jenneth couldn't endure any more.

'Look at the time,' she commanded huskily. 'You've got to be at the airport in time for the flight...'

They both moved away from the window as Jenneth went to take Louise's going-away outfit off the hanger, and neither of them saw the shadow cast by the motionless figure of the man standing directly beneath it.

He had gone into the rose garden intending to have a private and very forthright word with his daughter about the embarrassment she was causing both Jenneth and himself in attaching herself to Jenneth, but, as he was the first to admit, there were times when Angelica could wind him round her little finger. The tears that had immediately sprung to her eyes had only increased the guilt he already felt, and when she pulled away from him, her face streaked with tears of pride and anger, he had let her go.

He hadn't intended to linger in the garden, but the sound of Jenneth's voice had drawn him, and then, when he had realised what she was saying...

Angelica, who had been watching for her father with wary eyes, was astonished when he came up to her and ruffled her hair with a teasing grin, asking her if she had managed to get hold of any confetti.

Hesitantly she told him that Jenneth had promised to share hers with her, half expecting to see his smile banished by a frown, but instead his smile had widened and he had said in a way that made her feel that he was laughing, inside, 'Well, we'd better make sure that we find her, so that she can keep her promise, hadn't we?'

He was good as his word, and Jenneth, who had hoped to avoid him in the crush waving the married couple off, was disconcerted when he suddenly materialised at her side, saying as easily as he might have done nine years ago, when there were no bitter memories between them, 'Angelica tells me you've promised to share your confetti with us.' And then he picked up the little girl who was standing between them, watching them. Before Jenneth could move he stepped into the space Angelica had left, so that his dark suit-clad shoulder pressed against her as she turned to offer Angelica her box of confetti, and for a moment she was held immobile by the full impact of the green eyes as they studied her openly and thoroughly. Then, as the crowd surged around them and the breeze teased the silken strands of her hair, uncovered now that she had discarded her hat, he reached out and tucked the errant strands behind her ear.

The gesture was as familiar to her as her own face, and it froze her to a tension so obvious that the hand touching her hair stilled, its fingertips resting for the space of a heartbeat against her face in a gesture that, shockingly, seemed to offer comfort.

Jenneth withdrew from it as though scorched, causing Angelica to stare from her father to her new friend with puzzled eyes, sensing the awareness that seethed silently between them but too young to understand the cause of it. Then her attention was caught by the emergence of the bride and groom as they laughingly prepared to run the gamut of friends and relatives, gathered along the path to the front gate.

'They're here,' she told Jenneth excitedly, delving into the box of confetti, and in the ensuing disturbance Jenneth was able to step back and put a safe distance between herself and Luke.

When Louise reached her, she stopped and hugged her affectionately, producing a thin, square tissue-wrapped parcel which she handed to Jenneth with a grin...and a wicked smile which Jenneth only understood later, as she whispered to her, 'An unofficial thank-you for my unofficial bridesmaid, which reminds me...hold yourself in readiness to become a godmama...'

She saw the surprise in Jenneth's eyes and shook her head laughingly. 'No, not yet, stupid...but soon, we both hope.'

And then she was gone, bustled into the car by her protective bridegroom.

Jenneth waited until it had disappeared before turning away. Luke and Angelica were still beside her. She had hoped that by now they would have gone, and her heart quailed as she saw Louise's mother approaching them with a determined look.

'Jenneth, I'm so glad you're still here...I know you're staying at the Feathers overnight. We're having a small get-together here this evening, and of course we'd love you to join us.'

Despairingly Jenneth shook her head. She could not endure another minute of her present agony...

That horribly evocative touch of Luke's hand against her skin had awakened memories that were still making her pulses jerk and her blood run hot and giddyingly fast.

'I'm sorry, I can't,' she apologised, fibbing wildly. 'I promised the boys I'd ring them, and besides, it's a family affair...'

She couldn't look at Louise's mother as she made her escape, offering disjointed excuses for her refusal of her invitation...all too uncomfortably conscious of the small stir of interest caused by her departure.

Mrs Craven, the landlady of the Feathers, was obviously surprised to see her back so early. They were very busy in the dining-room, she announced regretfully, otherwise she would have invited Jenneth to tell her all about the wedding, adding that she had managed to slip out for just long enough to see the bride and groom emerge from the church.

'I saw you standing with Luke,' she said, adding, 'That little girl of his is a real character, isn't she? Pity about her mother dying when she was so young...'

To Jenneth's relief, before she could say any more a harassed waitress appeared in the foyer to announce that there seemed to be a mix-up with the booking for one of the tables, and Mrs Craven had to excuse herself.

Jenneth went up to her room and unlocked the door. Outside the sun was still warm, casting long early-evening shadows over the courtyard. Tiredly, Jenneth leaned against the window, trying to ease the tension from her body. Her head was starting to pound with the onset of a sick headache, reminding her that she had barely eaten a thing all day. Even now the thought of food made her shudder with revulsion, an unwelcome reminder of the dangerous decline in her health after Luke had broken off their engagement, when her weight had plummeted to such an extent that her parents had been seriously concerned for her. Before that she had been softly plump, but even after she had started eating normally again she had never regained her previous weight, so that people who knew her now remarked enviously on the slenderness of her narrow-boned body.

The room felt hot and stuffy, and she opened the window, breathing in the fresh air thankfully, shuddering a little as she remembered how inadvertently she had breathed too deeply when Luke was standing next to her and had been instantly aware of the frightening familiarity of his personal, intimate scent. She shuddered in the soft breeze blowing in through the window, her body suddenly drenched in sweat...

As her fingers curled protestingly in denial of what she was experiencing, she realised that she was still holding the present Louise had given her. She stared at it blankly, and then forced herself to walk over to the bed and unwrap it.

The thin, square, silver-foil package inside the tissue-paper bore the name of a very exclusive London shop that she recognised from high-fashion magazines... Puzzled, she removed the silk ribbon closing it and frowned over its mysterious tissue-wrapped contents.

As she removed the tissue-paper, a sharp, shocked gasp of protest left her lips as she saw what Louise had chosen to give her.

Inside the tissue paper was a nightdress...a nightdress such as Jenneth had never worn in her life, nor could ever envisage herself having the occasion to wear.

She picked it up with numb fingers, the fine, pale grey silk satin slithering coolly through her fingers as she stared at the tiny, fragile bodice of satin and lace, and the thin, delicate shoestring straps that supported it. Satin-covered buttons like those on Louise's chemise fastened the nightdress from floor-length to the top of the bodice, and it was cut, Jenneth realised, on the bias, so that it would mould and cling to whoever wore it, faithfully outlining every soft curve.

Jenneth stared at it in disbelief, wondering what on earth had prompted Louise to buy such a thing for her of all people, when she knew quite well that Jenneth was never likely to have the need or occasion to wear it.

In a sudden paroxysm of grief and rage, she balled it up in her hands and flung it across the room, before dropping face-down on the bed and howling like an angry child, muffling the impassioned force of her misery in the softness of the old-fashioned bolster pillow.

At her age she ought to have learned that the relief of bursting into tears was far outweighed by the destruction it caused, Jenneth recognised half an hour later as she surveyed her puffy face and pink eyelids with a grimace of self-disgust.

The bedroom, to which she had fled as a haven of escape from Luke and the memories seeing him conjured up, now seemed oppressively claustrophobic. She glanced at her watch. It was only just gone eight o'clock...

If she left now, she could be home in four or five hours, but caution reminded her that she was not really in any fit state to drive, and that the emotional trauma of the day had taken a severe toll on her.

Thanks to Luke, she was imprisoned alone in her hotel bedroom when she ought to have been forgetting the past and celebrating Louise's wedding with Louise's family, but how could she have joined them when she was so unbearably conscious of Luke and the frighteningly powerful effect he still had on her?

Beyond the roofs of the courtyard buildings she could just see the silver gleam of the river. Impulsively, she stripped off the expensive linen jacket and silk dress she had bought for the wedding, and changed into the jeans and cotton top she had driven down in.

No one paid any attention to her as she left the Feathers through a back door that opened on to the courtyard.

The village was quiet and empty as she made her way towards the river, and she silently blessed the fact.

The river had always drawn her; one of the things she loved about York was its river. Her parents' house overlooked the Ouse, and when the boys were teenagers the three of them had spent many a happy Sunday afternoon fishing for tiddlers.

She stopped dead where she stood, blindly oblivious to her surroundings, remembering against her will that it had been Luke who had taught her to fish, exhibiting all the patience and thoroughness that she suspected must make him the formidable surgeon she had learned from Louise that he had become.

Luke, Luke, Luke... her every sense had been filled by him all day, even before she had looked up during the ceremony and seen him standing there looking back at her.

She started to walk again, her movements uncoordinated and clumsy, almost running towards the river as though she were trying to outrun her own thoughts.

If she had thought that the river's placid flow would soothe her, she soon discovered that she was wrong. The sight of a pair of lovers entwined beneath the familiar canopy of the willows brought back too many heart-wrenching memories.

Once she and Luke had stood there like them... once Luke had held and kissed her, and she had kissed him back with innocence and desire, believing every promise he made her... believing that all the happiness in the world was hers. But it had all simply been an illusion, and she had been left with nothing.

Luke at least had his daughter, even if he had lost his wife, and deep inside her the ache intensified and Jenneth knew that there were some wounds that could never heal... Looking into the green eyes Angelica had inherited from Luke, Jenneth had bitterly envied the woman to whom Luke had given his child... the child he had once promised her.

CHAPTER FOUR

JENNETH had asked to be woken at seven so that she could make an early start back to York, and when the brief rap came on the door she was already awake.

She had breakfast in her room, studiously avoiding looking out of the window towards the river, and was just finishing her packing when someone rapped briefly on her bedroom door and opened it.

The sight of Luke framed there, dressed like her in jeans and a T-shirt, stunned her so much that all she could do was stand there and stare at him.

Dressed casually, he looked so much like the Luke she remembered that it took an immense effort of will not to reach out to him.

His glance took in her frozen stance and the overnight bag already packed, and then moved back to her, and for a moment his eyes seemed to darken with an emotion that freed Jenneth from her shock, projecting through her body a violent desire to repudiate that brief lightning glance of pity. How dared he pity her? How dared he knock on her bedroom door and simply walk in as though...?

'I'm glad I'm in time to catch you,' he was saying easily. 'Angelica was worried that you'd leave before she'd had time to say goodbye.'

His easy, friendly manner was so different from the cool indifference with which he'd treated her outside the church that Jenneth couldn't understand it.

'You brought Angelica here at this time of the morning?' she demanded huskily, her brain prompting the right responses while her body fought for survival.

'We're staying here,' Luke told her, frowning slightly, and then added softly, 'It's a pity you couldn't make it for dinner last night...' And the way he looked at her made Jenneth's heart pound with sick disbelief.

She blinked fiercely, terrified that she was beginning to imagine things that weren't there, and that she had somehow or other transposed into the present the Luke she had known in the past. But when she looked at him again she saw that the whimsical, gentle warmth still lit his eyes and that his mouth was curling upwards with the rueful humour that she remembered so poignantly.

'Jenneth, there's something I want to tell you...'

She stared at him uncomprehendingly, and heard him curse softly under his breath, and then say unsteadily, 'Oh, hell, don't look at me like that...'

And then, as the hot, betraying colour flooded her skin, Angelica erupted into the room, saying quickly, 'Daddy, is she still here?'

Jenneth's powers of self-defence sprang up inside her; she picked up her case with one hand, hugging Angelica briefly to her, unable to resist the impulse to give back the warm kiss the little girl gave her so enthusiastically, and escaped while she still had the ability to do so.

Luke watched her go with a wry look in his eyes, while Angelica complained, 'I wish Jenneth had been able to stay longer... I wanted to tell her about us going to live in York, Daddy, because that's where she lives...'

'I know,' Luke agreed absently, his keen eye caught by the sliver of grey satin lying on the floor. He walked over to it and picked it up, and a slow smile curled his mouth as he studied it...

'What's that?' Angelica asked him inquisitively.

'A nightdress,' he told her, adding with something approaching amusement, 'Jenneth's nightdress.' And then, bending to pick his small daughter up in his arms, he asked her, 'How would you like it if next weekend we went to York and took it back to Jenneth?' never for one moment doubting what his daughter's response would be.

She didn't disappoint him, responding with such enthusiasm that he laughed, and Angelica, who was unused to the sound of her father's untrammelled laughter, looked uncertainly at him.

Jenneth arrived home mid-way through Sunday to discover the twins waiting for her, together with a full-scale traditional Sunday lunch which they had cooked themselves. Her stomach churned nauseously as she smelled the roasting meat; the very last thing she wanted to do was to sit down and eat. Given a choice, she would much have preferred to escape to her studio and to stay there until she felt sufficiently in control of herself to face the rest of the world.

Seeing Luke when she had been so unprepared for the confrontation had reopened all the old wounds. The cool indifference with which his eyes had registered her presence and then dismissed it reminded her too sharply of the way he had looked at her when he had told her that he could no longer marry her.

Then, disbelieving and bewildered, she had denied what she was hearing, crying out that he couldn't mean it. His face had turned white, she remembered, the bones standing out in hard relief, and as she had gone towards him he had fended her off, taking her wrists in such a cruelly painful grip that she had actually cried out in pain.

That pain, though, had been nothing to compare with the other, deeper pain he had caused her... A pain which had never truly been vanquished, she admitted now, as she forced herself to smile and praise the twins for their efforts.

Looking up in church, and seeing Luke standing there watching her so clinically and emotionlessly, had brought home to her so sharply how vulnerable she felt as a woman; and as she sat down at Nick's bidding and accepted a glass of wine she really didn't want, while Kit made a dry, teasing comment about her single state and their chances of getting her married and off their hands before they left for university, she acknowledged that for her there could never be a relationship that might lead to marriage, because Luke had destroyed forever her own ability to believe herself worthy of being loved. With a sudden, piercingly bitter shaft of insight, she recognised that the hatred she ought to have turned outwards towards Luke she had turned inwards upon herself.

She shivered, and Nick, who was busy carving the meat, exchanged a concerned look with his twin.

Both of them knew that Jenneth had once briefly been engaged to Louise's cousin, but neither of them were aware of the true circumstances surrounding the ending of the engagement, and both of them had always assumed that it had been by mutual agreement... Now, silently, both of them asked one another what had happened at Louise's wedding to send their sister back looking as though she was about to collapse.

Looking up just in time to catch the concerned glances they exchanged, Jenneth forced herself to smile. She had grown so used to being responsible for her brothers, to protecting them and loving them, that she instinctively sought to hide from them her own pain and confusion.

She forced herself to talk about the wedding, telling them how surprised she had been by the un-Georgeiness of Louise's bridegroom. She told them that Louise and her parents all sent their love, and that Louise and George were going to try and pay them a fleeting visit later in the year.

In fact, she talked all through lunch, but never once mentioned Luke's name, stumbling only once, when she was describing how Angelica had handed her her handkerchief, biting her lip sharply as she remembered how the little girl had gone on to attach herself to her.

Nick and Kit, seeing the small, betraying gesture, said nothing but watched her worriedly.

After lunch, Jenneth told herself that she had wallowed in self-pity for long enough, and that if she was stupid enough to let herself get into such an emotional turmoil over a man who had cold-heartedly rejected her in favour of someone else, then she deserved all the anguish she was undoubtedly going to suffer; firmly she turned her mind to other matters, reminding the twins that they still had to come to a joint decision on whether or not to sell the house.

'We've already discussed it,' Kit told her promptly, acting as spokesman. 'And we don't want to sell . . . This house is our home, Jen,' he told his sister urgently. 'OK, so we're going away to university, but we'll be coming back . . .'

'If we sold, you'd both get a very useful lump sum of cash,' Jenneth reminded them, but they both shook their heads in unison.

'If money really is tight, you could always take in a lodger.' Nick told her thoughtfully, adding with a look at his brother that Jenneth intercepted and recognised, 'As a matter of fact, we've got a new teacher at school looking for somewhere to stay. Mr Alderson . . .'

Jenneth, who had come to recognise the moves her brothers made when they were trying to matchmake on her behalf, made an explosive sound in her throat, her emotions caught somewhere between laughter and tears.

'Look, you two,' she told them tartly, 'if . . . and I mean if . . . I should ever want to find myself a man, I'm perfectly capable of doing it—*myself* . . .'

She had learned years ago that where the twins were concerned only blunt speaking served any useful purpose, and she spoke as forcefully as she could, ignoring the small, mocking voice inside her that told her she was lying, especially if her past experience was anything to go by.

After another mutually exchanged glance, Kit told her wryly, 'Then why don't you?' And then, seeing her face, he got up and put his arm around her awkwardly, saying, 'Sis, it isn't that we want to get rid of you. It's just . . . it's just that we both think you need someone of your own. Some people need to be married,' he carried on, finding it difficult to vocalise the instinctive knowledge both he and his twin shared . . . 'You're not like Louise . . .'

'Thanks,' Jenneth told him shakily. 'What am I, then? A dependent, clinging vine who can't exist without a big strong man to lean on?'

Nick grinned—his sister was almost stubbornly independent when it came to practical matters, much more so than either he or Kit, but emotionally . . . well, that was a different matter entirely.

Jenneth was made for giving love and sharing it. They only had to see the way people responded to her . . . the way their friends responded to her . . . She had a gentle warmth that drew people, and she nurtured them, but they were too male and too young to be able to put what they felt into words. Jenneth meanwhile told them as forcefully as she could that, although the suggestion of taking in a lodger was potentially a good one, not so much from a financial point of view as from one of providing some alternative human companionship once the boys had gone, she was perfectly capable of finding such a lodger herself.

'I know you mean well,' she told them. 'But please try to understand . . . I'm happy as I am . . .'

After they had cleared lunch away and Jenneth had gone across to her studio, Kit looked ruefully at his brother and Nick said defensively, 'Well, I don't care what she says; she isn't happy.'

*   *   *

They weren't the only ones to think so. Eleanor, asking interestedly the following Wednesday how the wedding had gone, received such a brittle and uncommunicative response that she glanced thoughtfully at Jenneth's shadowed face and gently changed the subject, asking her if she had heard the news yet about the new appointment at the hospital.

Jenneth shook her head. Eleanor was involved in several charities, including the one that raised funds for the hospital, and was a fund of witty but never malicious items of local gossip.

'Well, you know that Harry Philips has had to retire...'

Jenneth nodded. Harry Philips was the chief surgeon at the hospital where she had been commissioned to paint the mural, and was well-liked in the local community. Five years off retirement age, he had suffered a heart attack earlier in the year, and had hoped to be able to go back to work.

'Mmm... Well, he has, and the man who's taking over arrives next week. He's fairly young, apparently. A real high-flyer. There's even a whisper that he's over-qualified for the job.'

Jenneth gave her a perfunctory smile. She wasn't really interested in the hospital's new appointee, save that he reminded her of Luke. She wondered a little bitterly if he realised the havoc he had caused within her... or cared.

She had woken up at three o'clock in the morning, with his name on her lips and the taste of her own tears in her mouth, and, as she dragged herself out of the pervading miasma of unhappiness and fought to deny the hopeless sense of loss and pain that had come with the dream, she had remembered how Luke had looked at her in her hotel bedroom. She trembled, trying to deny the vision, so that Eleanor, who was dismayed by the weight she could see Jenneth had lost, and the pain she could see she was enduring, ached to ask her directly what was wrong. But she knew Jenneth too well to do so. One direct question and Jenneth would close up like a clam.

She had no idea why it was that her friend and partner held the male sex at such a distance, but she had her suspicions, and later on, after Jenneth had left, and her own lover had telephoned to cancel a date they had for the evening, she cursed the male sex under her breath and wondered wryly if the female sex would not after all live happier lives had they been designed by nature as hermaphrodites and not one half of a whole whose completion seemed to cause so much trauma and pain.

Next morning, Jenneth, who had an appointment with a potential client who had recently moved to York and who wanted Jenneth to design and paint a mural for her small daughter's room, drove out of York and into the fertile valley of the Ouse. For once the beauty of her surroundings failed to supply balm to her soul... If by some miracle she could have wiped her memory clean of the weekend and Luke, she would gladly have done so.

Half-way to her destination, she pulled her car off the road and turned off the engine, acknowledging the truth she had been fighting against admitting ever since Louise had voiced it in the privacy of her bedroom.

She still loved Luke.

It was a long time before she felt able to restart the car and continue with her journey. Luckily she had some time in hand, and the prospective client turned out to be a pleasant and very friendly woman in her early thirties, who told Jenneth ruefully that she and her daughter were already in disagreement about what form the mural was to take.

Jenneth was used to dealing with this kind of problem, and the professionalism she had won for herself over the years took over, subduing the anguish of knowing that nothing had changed, that in so many ways she was still that same girl of twenty who had loved so readily and intensely. She acknowledged that she was no more able to cope with the reality of Luke's rejection now than she had been then.

She smiled, sympathetic to the client's plight, and suggested as tactfully as she could that it might be a good idea if she found out exactly what it was her daughter wanted. She had learned over the years that a compromise between the ideas of mother and child normally worked best, and after giving her a relieved smile Mary Andrews bustled away to call in her daughter, returning with a scowling girl of around Angelica's age, who although physically bearing no resemblance to Luke's child, brought back for Jenneth all the agony she had endured not just over Luke's rejection, but in knowing that another woman carried his child, and that that child was so instantly lovable and loving that Jenneth's envy of her dead mother had instantly increased.

Emma Andrews announced importantly that she knew just what she wanted. Jenneth made notes, and tactful, gentle suggestions that won grudging approval from Emma, and pleased relief from her mother.

Promising that she would prepare sketches of the mural and submit them to her just as soon as she could, Jenneth took her leave.

As she knew from bitter experience, the only way she had of coping with the pain inside her was to immerse herself so fiercely in her work that it and the exhaustion that sprang from it acted as a form of anaesthetic.

The twins and Eleanor watched her anxiously, knowing there was something wrong but unable to breach the defensive wall Jenneth had thrown up around herself.

On Saturday, despite the twins' objections, she announced that she was too busy to take any time off, and at nine o'clock in the morning she left for York and the hospital.

If the week had done nothing else, it had given her some ideas for the mural for the wall in the children's ward, and she wanted to spend the morning checking the ward and its light sources to see if her ideas would work.

One of the ideas she had in mind was a cartoon-type mural depicting children like themselves being helped by doctors and nurses. She wanted to show the patients in the mural getting well and healthy, and she wanted to talk over her ideas with the sister in charge of the ward. Were it not for the problems with the rapid turnover of staff, she would have contemplated using the actual features of the nurses and doctors for her cartoon figures, to add to their air of familiarity.

The sister in charge was a calm, smiling girl in her mid-twenties, who waved aside Jenneth's apologies for interrupting what was obviously a very busy schedule to say easily that nothing that helped the welfare of her patients, be it physically or mentally, was ever a waste of time.

Jenneth explained to her what she planned to do, and added that she intended to use the other walls in the ward to display more traditional murals, confessing that what made her task more difficult was the wide variation in ages of the children.

The discussion took longer than she had expected; the ward was a cheerful place, despite the seriousness of some of the children's illnesses, and it was gone twelve o'clock when she left.

The heatwave that seemed to have engulfed the country was continuing, and Jenneth sighed enviously as a sports car overtook her, its hood down, the driver's hair tousled by the slipstream.

She had enough material now to start work on some preliminary sketches, and her head was buzzing with what she intended to do as she drove down the rutted lane and then pulled into her own drive.

The house was only a mile from the village, but because it was set back off the main road it seemed more remote than it actually was.

The first thing she saw in front of the house was a gleaming and very obviously brand new slate-grey Jaguar car.

She eyed it a little enviously as she switched off her own engine, surmising that it belonged to the parents of one of the twins' friends, and reflected that, had it been her car, she would have been a little reluctant to lend so tempting a vehicle to so young a driver.

She half expected to see the twins and their friend in the garden, but as she walked up the side of the house towards the back door she saw that it was empty.

The lawn, liberally sprinkled with daisies and buttercups that she couldn't bring herself to destroy, was half mown, the mower abandoned. As she walked into the kitchen she heard male laughter, and grimaced to herself as she saw that the coffee-jug was empty, removing it from its stand and automatically replenishing the filter.

She heard the sitting-room door open, and through the open kitchen door heard Kit saying warmly, 'Jen's back . . . we'd better go and give her the good news . . .' And then the twins walked into the kitchen, closely followed by Luke and Angelica.

The glass jug for the coffee machine slipped out of her nerveless fingers and splintered noisily on the hard, tiled floor.

In shocked disbelief she stared over the twins' heads at Luke, who was standing motionless in the darkness of the doorway, his expression totally unreadable . . .

Luke here . . . why? What did he want?

While her pulse-rate fluctuated frantically, and Angelica, oblivious to her tension, darted forward to greet her, she dragged her gaze away from Luke's shadowed, enigmatic expression and automatically moved forward to prevent Angelica stepping on the broken glass.

Kit, who had already started to clear away the broken shards, berated her mildly for her clumsiness, and under cover of the general hubbub her gaze was drawn back to Luke, a dark, shadowy presence in a formal pin-striped business suit and a white shirt whose cuffs and front gleamed ghostly white in the darkness of the doorway.

'Jen, you never told us Luke's news...'

Luke's news... She focused on Nick's face, and it was like swimming through heavy seas, against a drowning tide. She seemed to have slipped from reality to a semi-conscious state where only the shock of Luke's presence was real.

Angelica wriggled in her arms and told her reproachfully, 'I wanted to tell you last weekend, but you left...'

She tried to concentrate on what was being said—on Angelica's sharp, piping voice, on the twins' deeper male tones but all the time it was Luke who filled her senses and her perceptions. Her heart was beating far too rapidly, and she was breathing shallowly, as though her chest hurt.

Her mouth had gone dry and her body was clenched tensely as she tried to fight off the effects of her shock.

And then, urbanely and calmly, as though it was the most natural thing in the world, Luke told her.

'I'm sorry our arrival is such a surprise, but in view of my predicament, and Aunt Caroline's suggestion that you might be able to help, I thought it best to come and see you personally...'

Aunt Caroline? What had Louise's mother to do with Luke's presence here? She looked wildly into his face and then heard Kit saying eagerly, 'It couldn't have worked out better if we'd planned it, Jen... Luke's moving up here to work at the Memorial Hospital. He's taking over there from next week, and he and Angelica need somewhere to stay until he can find himself a house. Louise's mother suggested that we might be able to put them up here, and of course we've told him there's no problem... After all, we've got bags of room, and since you're here most of the time you'll be able to keep an eye on Angelica for him... Couldn't be better, really,' Kit added, and then he turned to Luke and told him with a grin, 'Only this week we were telling Jen that she ought to take in lodgers when we go to university. We're not that far from the village, but neither of us likes the idea of her living here alone.'

Jenneth badly needed to sit down. She couldn't believe what she was hearing. Luke had calmly come up here and somehow or other convinced the twins that *she* would have no objection to Angelica and him moving in with them.

'Of course, we'll have to come to some mutually agreeable financial arrangement,' she heard Luke saying smoothly to her, and then, to Kit, 'and as for Jenneth taking charge of Angelica...your sister has a very busy career, and I hardly think it fair to inflict the responsibility of my daughter on her.'

'Oh, Jen won't mind,' Nick assured him breezily, breaking into the conversation. 'She loves kids. We keep telling her that she ought to get married and have half a dozen of her own...'

Angelica, still standing at her side, looked up at Jenneth and said blissfully, 'Isn't it the bestest thing ever? I told you last weekend that I wanted you to be my pretend mummy.' And Jenneth stared helplessly across the length of the kitchen to meet the knowing, amused look in Luke's eyes, and knew that she was quite helplessly and hopelessly trapped.

It took most of what was left of the afternoon to sort out the details. Luke was to take up his new appointment from the beginning of the month, only a week away. He had no idea how long it would take him to find not just a house but a housekeeper suitable to take charge of Angelica for him, he admitted, watching Jenneth's reaction with unnervingly astute eyes.

That was no problem, Kit assured him easily. He could take as much time as he liked, and Angelica, who was already half-way to hero-worshipping the twins, gave him an adoring, gratified look that reminded Jenneth unbearably of her own younger self and her adoration of Luke.

As she listened to the plans and decisions being made all around her, she kept on asking herself why on earth Luke should want to stay here with them. It was Angelica who unwittingly supplied the answer, by revealing that she had told Louise's mother how disappointed she was because Jenneth had gone home so quickly, and that it had been Louise's mother who had suggested to Luke that it might be worthwhile him getting in touch with Jenneth to see if she could help out with his accommodation problems, especially as Angelica had already established such a strong rapport with her.

Sick with anger and pain, Jenneth thought she could understand all too well what had motivated Luke. He was quite cold-bloodedly using her as an unpaid nanny for his child, and there was not a damn thing she could do about it... The twins were plainly delighted with the arrangement, seeing in Luke's presence the answer to their fraternal concern... To them, Luke was simply Louise's cousin... Jenneth doubted that they even remembered that she and Luke had once been engaged, and it was obvious that they had no idea just what they were doing to her by warmly inviting Luke to move in with them.

She herself was lost for words. She knew that if she looked directly at Luke, if she spoke to him, she would be in danger of breaking down completely, and all the pain and self-betrayal would pour out from her heart and destroy her. She couldn't bear to reveal to him how very vulnerable she still was, how she still ached from the pain of losing him, of being betrayed by him... How it affected her to see him with Angelica... How simply to look at him aroused such sensations of despair and need within her that she couldn't endure to stand there a moment longer.

She wanted to deny the twins' invitation to him, to break through his implacable expression and make him see the cruelty of what he was doing to her, but to do that would be to reveal that she still loved him, and that was something she simply could not bring herself to do.

She was trapped and she knew it. Despairingly she turned to Kit and said that she'd take Angelica upstairs and show her her room, but to her dismay Kit grinned at her and said, 'No need. We've been all through that... Luke's going to have the room next to yours. It's the only one with a double bed, and there's no way he'd be able to sleep in one of the singles in the other two rooms...'

'And I'm going to have the little room with the funny window,' Angelica interrupted importantly before Jenneth could say a word.

Luke sleeping in the room next to her own...the room which had been their parents'.

Forcing a tight smile to her stiff face, she said jerkily, 'I've got some work to do...' And before anyone could argue with her she picked up her sketch-book and fled to her studio.

Once there she made no attempt to work. How could she? Shivering with reaction, she stood staring out across the fields, wondering how the Luke she had once known—the Luke who had always cared so deeply about other people's feelings, had had such an awareness of them, such a compassion for others that she had ached to emulate him—could have changed into someone who could so indifferently cause her such pain.

Breaking their engagement was one thing... His betrayal of her was something she had made herself accept only by reminding herself that he had fallen in love with someone else, and that in so doing hurting her had been unavoidable, but this...this intrusion into her life...this cool assumption that she would not mind...this callous disregard of any needs other than his own...

Knowing that she could never truly have known him should have released her from the bondage of loving him, but it didn't.

She shuddered under the grip of the emotions that racked her, whirling round, defensively seeking the shadows as the studio door opened, admitting the strong summer sunlight and Luke's tall, commanding presence.

CHAPTER FIVE

FOR a moment neither of them spoke, and then Luke said with unforgivable duplicity, since she suspected he must know quite well how little she wanted him in her home, 'I'm very grateful to you for offering us a roof over our heads, Jenneth.'

She couldn't let it go, but neither could she say what was in her heart, so she said tonelessly instead, 'The offer wasn't mine,' and waited, praying that he would give her the opportunity to rescind it.

But he didn't, merely lifting a querying eyebrow before coming towards her, pausing in front of the window to say approvingly, 'A good north light...ideal for your work.' He stood looking over the countryside, in a silence that for one shocking moment Jenneth almost felt held regret and remorse, but she knew that she was merely projecting on to him emotions that she wanted him to feel. He was incapable of feeling either remorse or regret, and in all probability had even dismissed from his mind how badly he had once hurt her.

'Angelica seems to have attached herself very firmly to you.'

The abrupt statement surprised her, as did the expression she saw on his face, but then of course he would feel concern for his child ... for the child of the woman he had loved in preference to her. Hardening her heart against the vulnerability she had glimpsed in the shadows of his eyes, she said curtly, 'She's looking for a mother-substitute...'

There was silence, until Luke said quietly, 'Yes, I know.' And then, as though following some train of thought of his own, he added easily, 'You've done an excellent job with the twins, Jenneth. Your parents would be justifiably proud of you—and them.'

For some reason, when she had been able to hold out against all the other torments he had inflicted, this last one proved too much, and she lashed out fiercely at him.

'Meaning what, exactly, Luke? That because you approve of the way I've brought up the twins you think I'm a suitable person to take charge of your daughter? Am I supposed to be flattered by that?' she demanded bitterly. And then, before he could answer, she told him fiercely, 'I don't want you here, Luke. I don't want you in my life and I don't want you in my home...'

For a moment she almost thought she saw pain darken his eyes. He took a step towards her and she felt a fierce thrill of rebellion engulf her, but almost instantly he had himself under control, and, ignoring her comments as though they had never been uttered, he reached to unlock the small case he was carrying and said lightly, 'Oh, before I forget... You left this behind you at the hotel last weekend.'

Jenneth wasn't looking at him. Through the open door of her studio she saw to her dismay that the village's most notorious gossip was just about to walk up to her studio, and she remembered with a stab of irritation that she had promised to look out some jumble for her for a local fund-raising event.

She had arrived just in time to catch Luke's drawling statement, and Luke, with his back to the door, had no idea that she was there as he removed the grey silk nightdress from his case. Sliding it through his fingers, he said softly to Jenneth, 'I found it on the bedroom floor after you'd gone.' He threw it to her, and Jenneth saw the lightning calculation gleam in her unwanted visitor's eyes and knew despairingly that within days the whole village would have heard about the incident, suitably embellished and interpreted.

'Sorry to interrupt you, Jenneth... But you did say you'd have some jumble.'

In other circumstances she could almost have laughed at the inimical frown Luke turned on the older woman, who was already eyeing both Luke and the nightdress speculatively and with such obvious relish that Jenneth felt sick inside.

She suffered a moment's savage temptation to pick up the nightdress and hand it over as jumble, but common sense stayed her, and instead, excusing herself to Luke, she escorted the other woman out of the studio and towards the garage, deflecting her unsubtle probing as best she could.

The day's only relief was the announcement by Luke that he was spending the weekend with a medical colleague and his wife. As she listened to the twins and Angelica chorusing their mutual disappointment, she could only pray despairingly that fate would relinquish its torment of her and speedily provide Luke with his own house.

It was only her own ingrained good manners and an awareness that both the twins and Angelica were watching her that enabled her to walk with Luke to his car while he told her blandly that, since he had a few days in hand, it seemed a pity not to take advantage of the good weather and further Angelica's education at the same time by joining the household part-way through the week, so that he would have time to spare to show Angelica the surrounding countryside before taking up his new post.

Jenneth gave him a tight smile, too engrossed in her own pain to see the sudden shadowing of his eyes as she forestalled his attempt to bridge the gap between them.

What had she intended to do? She wondered achingly. Kiss her goodbye? The same chaste salute on the cheek that she had seen him afford his aunt and Louise on countless occasions in the past?

'We won't keep you any longer,' he told her, his voice suddenly and unaccountably hard and unkind. 'It's Saturday, and no doubt you've got plans for the evening. I must say you've surprised me, Jenneth,' he added, and there was something in the way he looked at her that made her catch her breath and cringe inwardly beneath the subtle cruelty of his mocking voice. 'When you told me you'd embraced the mores of the sexual revolution and that you preferred the variety of a succession of lovers to the vegetation of one single stable relationship, I thought you were simply taking defensive measures, but here you are, twenty-nine years old, still single, still unwilling to commit yourself to one among your many lovers.'

As she winced beneath the gentle but oh, so destructive words, he opened the car door for Angelica, and then turned back to Jenneth and said, with a smile that was as cold and cruel as an arctic winter, 'Incredible—after so much and such varied sexual experience, you still manage to project that same air of virginal apprehension. If there's one thing I regret about the past, it's possibly that I wasn't your first lover.'

No one other than she could hear what he was saying, and she fought hard to control the crawling burn of colour that betrayed what she was feeling.

Caution warned her against retaliating, already knowing that the price of such a retaliation would be too high, but she was in no mood to listen to any cautionary voices and, almost stuttering with fury and pride, she turned to him and hissed virulently, her eyes turning from cool grey to dark, anguished purple, 'If there's one thing *I* regret, it's that I was ever stupid enough to believe you were anything other than a liar and a cheat...' Then, unable to withstand the overpowering temptation to pierce his obnoxious conceit, she added acidly, 'And as for being my lover—first, last or any other... I'd rather die...'

She was trembling as she stepped back from him, almost incoherent with rage and resentment, freed momentarily from the burden of her pain to the exhilaration of giving vent to emotions she had fought too long to control.

Giving him a final contemptuous glare, she turned her back on him, fierce quivers of sensation racing down her spine as she heard his soft laughter following her.

Naturally, for the rest of the weekend the twins were full of the convenience of the coincidences which had, so they believed, led to a more than satisfactory resolution of both their and Luke's problems.

'We were worried about leaving you here on your own,' Kit told Jenneth for the umpteenth time over dinner on Sunday evening. 'But now, with Luke here...'

Jenneth gritted her teeth and said nothing. She had stood in for their parents for so long that it was beyond her to destroy their illusions and tell them the truth... Watching her pick at her food, Kit and Nick exchanged guilty and conspiratorial looks above her downbent head and, as Kit confided to his twin later that evening when they were alone, if he wasn't convinced that Luke was doing the right thing, he didn't think he'd be able to endure Jenneth's misery.

'It *has* hit her pretty hard, hasn't it?' Nick agreed. 'But Luke's right. If he'd simply told her that he realised that he'd made a mistake, and that she was the one he'd wanted all along, she wouldn't have believed him...'

'No... I never realised he'd dumped her for someone else, did you?'

'He didn't have much choice, did he, not with the other girl pregnant? I suppose he had to do the decent thing...'

They exchanged wryly masculine looks, and Nick said uneasily, 'Makes you think, doesn't it?'

There was silence, and then Kit reflected, 'Just as well that Luke had time to tell us what the situation was before Jen got back. I was terrified she was going to tell him he couldn't stay when he announced that we'd invited him to move in...'

'Mmm, me too. Do you think she *does* still love him?'

Kit grinned at him and scoffed, 'Are you totally blind?'

His twin, always the more soft-hearted of them, was looking a little uncomfortable, and Kit guessed that he was worrying about whether or not they had done the right thing in allowing Luke to persuade them to join his conspiracy to get Jenneth to admit him back into her life.

'It's not going to be easy,' he had admitted bluntly. 'She has every reason to loathe and resent me.' And then he had told them coolly and very objectively what he had done.

'If you ditched her then, why should we believe you want her back now?' Kit had asked him equally bluntly, and he had given them a look that Kit later confessed to his twin had made him feel as though he had trespassed into very private territory indeed.

All he had said to them, though, was, 'I loved your sister then and I still love her now. For that I'm afraid you will have to accept my word.' And, oddly enough, for some reason that had been sufficient.

It was Nick who had thought to ask him just what he wanted from Jenneth, and he had replied promptly, 'Marriage...' Then he had added wryly, 'And somehow I think *that* will be easier to achieve than regaining her trust, so *that*, I'm afraid, must come first.'

A statement at which both of them had boggled a little, since Luke had not minimised how much Jenneth was bound to resent and mistrust him.

Even now they weren't quite sure just how Luke intended to persuade Jenneth to marry him, when by his own admission she neither liked nor trusted him.

'There are ways,' he had said mysteriously in response to their question, and then, before they could ask him any more, Angelica had come bursting in, demanding both their and her father's attention, and wanting to know when Jenneth was coming back.

'You don't think he'll hurt her, do you?' Nick muttered uncertainly, earning himself a cynical look from his twin and the response,

'Do you mean more than he has already?'

Jenneth was too preoccupied with her own thoughts to notice anything unusual in the twins' behaviour. There were practical matters appertaining to Luke and Angelica's arrival which kept her hands busy, as though she wasn't busy enough already.

Nick, wandering into her studio one Tuesday afternoon, noticed the silk nightdress screwed up on the floor, and picked it up, studying first it and then his sister with raised eyebrows.

'Louise gave it to me for being her unofficial bridesmaid,' Jenneth told him, anticipating his question.

'Mmm ... not exactly your style, it it?' he commented with a grin and a frankness that for some reason hurt. Even her brothers, or so it seemed, recognised that essential lack of sexual allure in her nature that had led to Luke discarding her in favour of someone else. 'What's it doing in here, anyway?' he asked curiously.

'I left it at the hotel and Luke brought it back for me,' Jenneth told him, deliberately turning her back on him so that he wouldn't see the telltale surge of colour running up her skin.

She had no way of knowing whether or not Laura Gosford had yet passed on details of the interesting scene she had witnessed, but if she had, and if either of the twins got to hear of it, it would be extremely awkward if she had fibbed to Nick about the reasons for the nightdress's presence on her studio floor.

Damn Luke, and damn Louise as well, she thought inwardly, watching the way her brother's eyebrows rose. If the nightdress weren't so blatantly provocative, if it were one of her normal plain cotton nightshirts, she was quite sure it would never have provoked the very obviously erroneous thoughts its presence in Luke's possession seemed to arouse.

Nick was grinning at her, and he came over to her and said teasingly, 'Come on, Jen, there's no need to be embarrassed. We're all grown-up now; if you and Luke are having a bit of a thing...'

Jenneth glowered at him.

'We aren't,' she told him flatly, then added anxiously, 'Nick ... please don't suggest anything like that to Luke, would you—not even in fun? It would be... embarrassing for both of us,' she explained.

'You mean because you were once engaged? But that was over years ago,' Nick protested cheerfully.

Then, seeing her face, he agreed, 'OK, I won't say anything, although you've got to admit, it's very suspicious. I mean, how did Luke know the nightdress was yours? How come you left it behind in the first place?'

Jenneth was thankful that the telephone rang, freeing her from her brother's teasing questions. She picked up the receiver, firmly turning her back on him and listening to Eleanor's wry complaint that she was finding life a little dull as her lover was away on business, and that she had decided to give a dinner party to enliven it a little.

'Naturally I want you to come, but what I also want is your recipe for that delicious fruit sauce you make.'

The dinner party was on Saturday and, confirming that she would be able to attend, Jenneth reeled off the details of the required recipe.

Sooner or later she was going to have to tell Eleanor about Luke...or rather about the fact that he was going to be staying with her. She bit her lip, gnawing worriedly at it. Her friend was far too perceptive at times, and Jenneth could only hope she would manage to give a convincing performance of Luke being nothing other than an old family friend.

He and Angelica were due to arrive in the morning.

In any other circumstances she would have delighted in the anticipation of Angelica's company, but the mere thought of Luke standing by and watching with coolly detached awareness of her vulnerability while she became enslaved by his child was enough to make her wish that Angelica was the kind of revoltingly spoiled and unappealing child she could easily and safely hold at a distance.

She was surprised that Luke, who very obviously loved his daughter, should not see the danger of Angelica forming an emotional attachment to her which must cause the little girl unhappiness when it eventually had to be broken.

Angelica was endearingly honest and open in her feelings, and in her desire for her father to remarry and provide her with a mother. Of course she had been very young, less than two and a half when her own mother had died, and she quite plainly adored her father and knew that he loved her in turn. Because of her own emotional make-up, it was plain that she felt no jealousy or resentment at the thought of sharing her father with someone else, possibly because she was too young as yet to be aware of adult emotions, and in her childish way she would see any second marriage that Luke contracted merely as her father's wish to provide her with the mother she so desperately wanted.

Would Luke marry again? Another sophisticated, experienced woman able to match and arouse his sexuality in a way that she with her naïveté had not?

Savagely she gritted her teeth, remembering the full measure of her own ignorance . . . remembering how she had assumed, because she naïvely had found just the mere touch of Luke's hand against her skin so intensely thrilling that she practically choked on the excitement of it, that Luke was similarly affected by the slightest intimacy with her, when in reality . . . She took a deep breath, and forced herself to confront the truth.

The reality was that Luke had never desired her enough to do more than make light-hearted imitation love to her, and when he felt real desire—real need—it had been for someone else.

And yet why, knowing that—and he must surely have known it well before he proposed to her—had he invited that sort of commitment? Male vanity... boredom?

Once she would have asserted that the Luke she knew could never behave so shallowly, but Luke himself had shown her how far she had mistaken his true nature.

So, knowing that, why did she still love him? Why did she still react to him as intensely and dangerously as she had done at twenty-one?

She had deliberately planned to be out when Luke arrived, firmly telling the twins that, since he was there at their invitation, they could be the ones to give up their time to welcome him.

Resolutely she filled her day with appointments, returning home well after the rush-hour traffic had emptied York, hoping against hope that something would have happened to prevent Luke's arrival.

It hadn't. The first thing she saw as she turned into the drive was his grey Jaguar. The second was Angelica, who was plainly waiting for her.

Despairingly she returned the little girl's enthusiastic hug, knowing she simply did not have what it took to reject her. Because she knew what that kind of rejection felt like?

'Daddy's making supper,' Angelica told her astonishingly. 'I'm starving, aren't you?' And then, as she danced at Jenneth's side, she added accusingly, 'I've been waiting ages and ages for you. I wanted you to come with me to see my new school, but Daddy said you were very busy. I told the teacher about you, though... I told her that you were my pretend mummy and I told her about Kit and Nick... I'd like to have some brothers,' she added wistfully. And Jenneth, too exhausted to say anything, followed her into the kitchen, startled to discover that she had spoken the truth and that Luke was preparing supper. An appetising smell of spices filled the kitchen, making her sharply aware that she hadn't eaten all day.

'Good, you're back,' announced Luke without looking at her. 'We checked on your last appointment and guessed that you'd be back around now. Hope you still like lasagne...'

Disbelief rendered her speechless as she digested his throwaway remark, and she wondered wrathfully which one of the twins it had been who had given him access to her diary and her telephone book.

'There was no need to wait for me,' she told him curtly, causing him to turn round and say softly,

'It wouldn't have been the same without you.'

She could feel her face burning as much with rage as with self-consciousness, and on an impulse she didn't want to name she told him savagely, 'Well, I'm afraid you've wasted your time. I'm eating out tonight.'

It was a lie, and for a moment, watching him, she actually thought he was going to say as much, but then Angelica tugged on her sleeve and implored, 'Can't you really have supper with us?'

Above his daughter's head Luke's eyes met hers.

If he had primed Angelica he couldn't have done better, she acknowledged, torn between resentment that he should walk into her home and her life and calmly expect her to accept him as though all the years of anguish and misery had never been, and reluctance to hurt the little girl watching her so pleadingly.

And then, to her surprise, he put down the spoon he was holding and came over to them, taking hold of Angelica and telling her gently, 'You heard Jenneth, Angie. She's already made arrangements to go out tonight.'

He stood up with Angelica in his arms, his eyes boring into hers with flat, biting accusation, and she wondered helplessly why it was that she should be made to feel guilty, when he was the one who was culpable.

The very last thing she wanted to do was to go out again, but she had no alternative now, so she went upstairs, showered and changed into a cool silk dress... redid her hair and make-up and went back down again to find Nick and Kit waiting for her to demand where she was going and with whom.

'I'm having dinner with a client...' she told them vaguely, and then stiffened when she heard Luke saying laconically behind her,

'There's no need to spare our feelings, Jenneth...' She swung round, glaring at him, and he added softly, 'Wearing an outfit like that, there's no way you're going out on a business date... and be-sides——' he added as Kit and Nick exchanged looks and quickly melted away. 'And besides, the twins have already told me that you never agree to business dinners or meetings in the evening.'

It was true. A self-imposed rule begun when the boys had been younger, and which she had automatically stuck to.

As she bit her lip in vexation, Luke asked idly, 'Will you be bringing him back here?'

She stared at him stupidly for a moment, and then said bewilderedly, 'Who?'

'Your date, of course...' He shrugged powerful shoulders, and unwisely her gaze clung to the hard breadth of his torso, her memory conjuring up a disturbing vision of a hot Sunday afternoon when they had lain on the riverbank and Luke had removed his shirt. His skin had been tanned and unexpectedly tempting to touch. He had laughed at her shyness and taken her hands and spread them over his body, holding them there and then moving them as he kissed her...

Her mouth went dry at the disturbing image.

'After all, we're both adults,' Luke was saying. 'And if you want me to make myself scarce, you only have to say so. I expect you found it difficult at first, getting the twins to accept that you had a fully functioning sex life. I must admit I'm dreading the time coming when Angelica starts asking awkward questions, and I suspect boys are ten times worse, especially when they're as protective as the twins are of you...'

Jenneth stared at him in disbelief, and without thinking said roundly, 'If you're intimating that I'd bring my dates back here...and go to bed with them...'

She stopped abruptly, realising what she was in danger of betraying, but to her relief Luke seemed unaware of her. He wasn't looking at her, and the dark lashes lowered over his eyes concealed his expression from her.

'Oh, you find it easier to go back to their place... Well, yes, I can see the sense in that.' He gave a rich chuckle, and told her, 'I can see I'm going to have to pick your brains while I'm staying here; I suspect you'll be able to give me plenty of useful tips...' A casual, easy smile was thrown her way, together with the breathtaking enquiry, 'Will you be away all night, or...?'

Jenneth compressed her mouth and said furiously, 'No, I shall not!'

'Mmm... Personally, when I make love I must admit I enjoy the intimacy of spending the entire night with my partner, but then I must admit I'm a little old-fashioned about these things, and my experience probably falls very far short of yours.'

'I doubt it,' Jenneth told him through gritted teeth, wondering what on earth she was going to do with herself all evening, and where she was going to go.

In the end she went to the gallery, let herself in with her own set of keys, and then rang Eleanor, relieved to find that her friend was spending the evening alone and only too delighted with her offer of company.

'This isn't like you,' she smiled, when she opened her front door to Jenneth an hour later. 'Normally nothing can prise you away from home in the evening. Anything wrong?' she added when she saw the high flush of colour of Jenneth's otherwise pale face, and the grim set of her mouth.

'I'm having a few problems at home,' Jenneth admitted, knowing that it was impossible to pretend that nothing was wrong.

'With the twins?' Eleanor asked in some surprise.

Jenneth shook her head and sat down. Suddenly she needed desperately to unburden herself to someone, and Eleanor at least was someone she could trust . . . someone detached enough from the situation to be able to understand.

She explained briefly, in a tight, controlled voice, about her engagement to Luke and his subsequent marriage to someone else, and then told Eleanor about his totally astounding arrival in York, and the twins' unintentional betrayal in inviting him to make a temporary home with them.

'Good heavens!' Eleanor said frankly. 'In view of the fact that he rejected you for someone else, I should have thought you'd be the last person he'd want to stay with . . .'

Jenneth shrugged and said frustratedly, 'It's almost as though he's trying to pretend that none of that ever happened. He behaves as though we're old friends . . . as though . . .' She gestured helplessly, trying to convey her despair and confusion.

'Why don't you just tell him firmly that you want him to leave?' Eleanor suggested mildly.

Jenneth shook her head.

'I can't,' she said huskily.

Eleanor gave a faint sigh and touched her arm lightly. 'Ah . . . now I think I begin to understand. What to him appears to be very much a forgotten incident, to you is still a painful and wounding issue . . .'

'Yes,' admitted Jenneth unhappily. 'And I'm afraid that if I try and tackle him I'll do or say something that will betray to him how I feel...'

'And how do you feel?' Eleanor asked her calmly.

Jenneth grimaced. 'Much as I did ten years ago when I first realised I loved him.'

'And you're frightened that he'll guess that? Surely, if he's treating the whole thing as though it never happened, he can't be astute enough to make that kind of assumption?'

Jenneth shook her head.

'No way,' she told Eleanor grimly. 'He's *very* astute.'

She missed the sharp, thoughtful glance Eleanor gave her, lifting her head only when Eleanor said humorously, 'Well, short of offering you sanctuary in the shape of one of my spare bedrooms, I don't know what I can do to help.'

'I can't do that,' Jenneth told her bitterly. 'Luke already believes I'm spending the evening with my lover. If I stay here, he'll probably tell the twins I'm spending the night with him.' She gave a soft shiver and added wryly, 'I'm supposed to be the guardian of their morals, and not the other way round, but...'

'Yes, but...' agreed Eleanor drily. 'It never ceases to amaze me that men can become so outraged at the thought of one of their own kind daring to see their mother and sisters as sexually available, when that is exactly what they are doing themselves to someone else's mother or sister...'

Jenneth laughed, and Eleanor said firmly, 'That's better...' She got up and said quietly, 'Jen, it's none of my business, but I suppose it hasn't occurred to

you to simply *ask* Luke why he's forcing himself
back into your life like this? You say he's an astute,
intelligent man; he must know how much he hurt
you. Most men would run a mile from a situation
such as the one he's deliberately got himself into...
They're all cowards at heart, and none of them likes
being reminded of those occasions in their lives
when they've behaved in a fashion that's less than
gentlemanly...'

Jenneth said tiredly, 'I expect that as far as he's
concerned, he did the right thing. She was, after
all, expecting his child...'

'A child conceived when he was actually engaged
to you,' Eleanor reminded her. She looked
worriedly at her friend and said consideringly, 'It
couldn't be, I suppose, that he regrets what he
did...that he's looking for a second chance?'

Jenneth stared at her, hope flaring fiercely inside
her, and then dying just as quickly.

'No,' she said firmly.

'Well, there's only one way you're going to find
out the truth,' Eleanor told her gently, 'and that's
by asking him...'

She was disturbed to see the bitterness glitter in
Jenneth's normally gentle eyes as she said tautly,
'Luke lied to me in the past...why should he tell
me the truth now? Anyway, I think it's just that he
sees me as a convenient "someone" to take care of
Angelica for him until he can get himself organised.'

Eleanor raised her eyebrows and said, 'I thought
you told me he loved his daughter.'

'He does,' Jenneth confirmed. 'Why?'

'Because, my dear, if he's astute as you seem to
think, and if he loves his child as you say he does,

then surely the very last person he'd want to entrust her to would be a woman who, by his own treatment of her, had the very best reason in the world for wanting to punish him and make him suffer as she'd suffered, and what better way to do that than through his child . . .'

'Oh, but I couldn't do anything like that,' protested Jenneth.

Eleanor smile grimly. 'No,' she agreed, and then warned, 'Be careful, Jenneth . . . I suspect he knows you better than you think.'

'But not well enough to realise that my nights are not filled with a never-ending succession of different lovers,' Jenneth told her, striving to sound light-hearted.

She glanced at her watch. It was only eleven o'clock. She dared not arrive home before one at the earliest.

'How would you like it if I spent a couple of hours working on the accounts?' she suggested to Eleanor.

CHAPTER SIX

IT WAS almost a quarter to two when Jenneth parked her car between the twins' Metro and Luke's Jaguar.

She was exhausted mentally and physically, her head pounding from two hours spent poring over columns of figures, her temper close to boiling point; her defence mechanism of distancing herself from anything approaching any kind of emotional reaction seemed to have completely deserted her.

She walked wearily into the kitchen, thinking only of crawling into bed and staying there, hopefully until Luke had ended his self-invited visit.

The kitchen light was on, and she grimaced a little. How often had she told the twins about wasting electricity? There had been times, especially as they grew fully into their teens, when it had often shocked her to hear the very strong echoes of their parents' voices in her chiding of her brothers.

'You're back. Good, I was just beginning to wonder if you'd changed your mind and had decided after all to stay over...'

Jenneth stiffened, staring in disbelief into the shadowy corner of the kitchen, where Luke was lazily uncoiling himself from the comfortable, if shabby, chair beside the Aga.

There was a book on the table beside him. She couldn't read its title upside-down, but it looked

like some kind of text-book. She noticed this
vaguely as the full force of all her resentment and
frustration boiled up inside her and she snapped
furiously, 'You're *not* my keeper, Luke. If I choose
to stay out all night that's no concern of yours, and
as for you lurking here in the kitchen waiting for
me as though . . . as though I was some kind of idiotic teenager, incapable of running my own life . . .'

'I agree.' The calm words silenced her, and she
stared at him, her chest heaving, her eyes wild with
anger that was dying to be replaced by an instinctive wariness.

'As a matter of fact, the twins were concerned
about you.' He gave her an oblique, almost knowing
look that made a fine chill of apprehension run over
her skin.

'They seemed to find it unusual and therefore
worrying that you should be staying out so late,
and so in order to ease their minds I offered to stay
up and check that you got in safely . . .'

There was nothing Jenneth could say. She
glowered at him in frustrated silence, all too aware
of the thinly veiled challenge he had just given her.
It hadn't been by accident that he had mentioned
the twins' surprise. Did he guess that she had lied?
That she had not spent the evening with a lover,
but on her own?

As this humiliating thought struck her, he asked
conversationally, 'Did you have a pleasant
evening?'

Jenneth looked suspiciously at him, but he had
retreated into the shadows and his voice held
nothing but polite, urbane enquiry.

'Very pleasant, thank you,' she said stiffly.

He moved then, and she saw the mocking, glittering smile that darkened his eyes as he taunted, 'Ah, Jenneth...how ungenerous you are. Were I your lover, I should feel very deflated indeed to hear an evening spent in my company described with such lacklustre words... Will you be seeing him again?'

The dulcet, dangerous question slipped so easily beneath her guard, causing her to jump and react with instinctive self-defence, fibbing wildly.

'Yes...on Saturday. We're having dinner together...'

Thank goodness she had Eleanor's dinner party to attend, and would not need to endure another long, exhausting evening in the gallery's cramped office, she reflected miserably, as she turned away from her tormentor and headed for the door.

Only somehow or other Luke was there before her, barring her way, with the intimidating barrier of his lean, hard body.

'I'd like to go to bed, Luke,' she objected sharply, her nerve-endings quivering suddenly at the way he was looking at her, studying the shape of her body under the thin covering of her silk dress...almost as though she was a long-awaited gift he was anticipating unwrapping, she recognised.

'Poor Jenneth,' he mocked her. 'Something tells me your evening wasn't the success you're trying to pretend. Perhaps this will make it better,' he suggested softly. And before she could move, she was trapped against the wall by the intimacy of his body with its heat and maleness, with nowhere to go other than into the arms he stretched out to entrap her.

That he should be doing this to her was so out of context, so unexpected, that by the time she had marshalled her wits and was pushing frantically at his chest he was already feathering his mouth along the soft, vulnerable flesh of her exposed jawline, whispering unbelievably in her ear. 'You used to like this... Do you remember?' And then, 'But of course, these days no doubt you prefer more sophisticated stimulation.' And his hands slid smoothly down her back to pull her into the heat of his body, so that the hard maleness of his flesh was imprinted against her, the fierce thud of his heart beating into her.

The mouth he lowered to cover her own was unexpectedly gentle, its pressure and seduction so dangerously reminiscent of the past, that her own mouth had softened and opened almost before she knew what was happening.

Even when she heard the soft sound of satisfaction buried in his throat, it didn't really register what was happening... It was all so totally unbelievable.

He kissed her slowly and tenderly, reducing her to a shivering, uninhibited responsiveness. The stunning incredulity of being in his arms, of being touched and kissed in that way, was so achingly familiar to her that her body was swept unthinkingly into response patterns so long ago set down that she had not even realised they were there.

She felt the hard arousal of Luke's body, and instinctively pressed closer to him, blindly seeking the intimacy of flesh on flesh contact.

She felt Luke tense, mutter something against her lips as they clung moistly to his, and then he was kissing her again, more urgently this time, demanding from her a response that she was only too eager to give.

She felt his hands on her back and the coolness of the air on her exposed flesh as he eased her dress away from her body, and then he was touching her breasts, sending shock-waves of sensation shuddering through her body as though her skin had caught fire.

She tensed and moaned beneath the disruptive caress, wanting him to go on, wanting him to fulfil the unspoken promises he had made her so long ago, when his touch had whispered seductively to her body that he would show it pleasure beyond imagining... Only he had not done so. Instead he had been sharing that pleasure with someone else.

Instantly she went cold, remembering where she was and with whom, and Luke, sensing her withdrawal, lifted his mouth from hers and watched her.

'I don't know what you think you're doing...' she began unsteadily, but he stopped her with a cruel, taunting smile that locked her breath in her throat.

'No?' he queried softly, with almost insolent amusement. 'I should have thought it was obvious.' His voice had dropped to a dangerously malevolent purr. 'Especially to a woman of your experience. I was attempting to give you the satisfaction your lover so obviously failed to supply.'

And the smile he gave her was at once so bland and so cruel that she felt she would freeze where she stood.

'Not a wise decision on second thoughts,' he added, monitoring every change in her expression, making her feel that she was exposed to him in the most dangerous and intimate way possible. 'And as acts of charity go, not a particularly successful one, either...'

Acts of charity... Jenneth felt her legs almost buckle beneath her.

A hot, searing tide of misery and loathing flooded into her, and she ached for the detachment and the cynicism to match him with the kind of loaded, barbed response that would damage him as he had just damaged her. But she couldn't think of a single thing to say, and so, turning on her heel, she wrenched open the kitchen door and made her way shakily to her bedroom.

Luke waited until the door had closed behind her, and then moved restlessly over to where he had left the medical text-book he had been reading.

His colleagues had been astounded when he had announced that he was putting in for this job, hiding himself away in an admittedly excellent but relatively unknown teaching hospital, when top hospitals the world over were clamouring for his skills as a surgeon. None of them had been able to understand his decision. They had thought he was mad and told him so. Now he wondered if they hadn't been right.

That had been an idiotic move, challenging her sexually like that... and if her initial response had been the sweetest pleasure he had known in years, it had been a pleasure quickly lost and it had left him with an ache that reminded him savagely that, no matter how intelligent, how educated, how analytical a man might teach himself to be, there were still times when his physical responses would always overwhelm his intellect.

He reached for his discarded book, and then swore softly under his breath as he saw how unsteady his hands were.

All he had achieved tonight for his impatience and physical need had been a few seconds of solace, followed by the knowledge that he had probably driven Jenneth well and truly behind her protective defences.

As he switched out the kitchen light, he wondered where she had actually spent the evening, and grimaced a little to himself. It might be necessary... but that didn't mean he had to like what he was doing. How much simpler to just go to her and tell her the truth. But he knew what would happen if he did.

She would hear him out, smile at him with that grave, distancing little smile, and then very coolly and firmly send him on his way. No, that was not the answer... in order to succeed, this battle must be conducted from inside her defences, not from outside them.

'Jenneth, is this a weed?' Angelica asked importantly, holding up a piece of chickweed for Jenneth's inspection.

Jenneth nodded, smiling a little at the little girl's absorption in their shared task of weeding the herbaceous border. The twins teased her about the way Angelica had attached herself to her, claiming with the unfair forthrightness of brothers that it only upheld their claim that Jenneth had missed her vocation in not marrying young and producing at least half a dozen children. Jenneth had firmly subdued their banter, because she was aware that beneath Angelica's fierce attachment to her lay a potentially serious problem.

It would be morally unfair to allow Angelica to become dependent on her emotionally, and yet to rebuff the child might cause equally deep psychological scarring; so Jenneth was fighting hard to maintain an attitude which, while allowing her to respond affectionately to the need she sensed within Luke's daughter, also allowed her to salve her conscience that she was not encouraging Angelica to form a dependence on her from which the little girl would suffer when inevitably they were parted.

The long-lasting heatwave had played havoc with the garden, and so Jenneth had given herself a well-deserved half-day off, and she and Angelica were spending it companiably attacking the weeds.

'I wish you and Daddy weren't both going out tonight,' she confided artlessly, and then added judiciously, 'I like Kit and Nick, but I love you and Daddy best...'

Jenneth's heart twisted. She wanted to remonstrate with her, to warn her that she must *not* love her, to tell her that such loving could only be dangerous, but she was so young and Jenneth knew she wouldn't understand...

'Daddy's going out with some friends, Jenneth; who are you going out with?'

Jenneth swallowed. It was one thing to lie to Luke in the heat of the moment, but quite another to lie to Angelica and the twins.

'A friend,' she said vaguely, directing Angelica's attention to a large patch of weeds in an attempt to deflect her questions.

The twins were out with some friends, and despite the fact that it was a Saturday, and he didn't take up his new appointment until the following week, Luke was at the hospital.

He would be a good surgeon, Jenneth reflected. He had the necessary clinical detachment for it. His mother would have been so proud of him. Jenneth remembered long-ago conversations with Luke about his aspirations...about his mother's deteriorating condition and his very evident frustration at not being able to do anything to halt it. She had been one of the warmest human beings Jenneth had ever known, bravely making light of her illness and the pain it caused her. Unlike Luke's father...a difficult, rather immature man who saw his wife's suffering only in terms of how it affected his life.

Jenneth remembered the uneasy relationship that had existed between Luke and his father. Too often she had seen Luke's mouth tighten as he had explained to her why it was necessary for him to break a date, telling her that his father was out somewhere and that he was reluctant to leave his mother on her own.

Luke's parents' marriage could not have been a happy one, but Luke's mother had never allowed her feelings to show. Even so, there had been whispers in the village about the doctor's attitude towards his wife: people admired her for her bravery and pitied her for her husband's weaknesses.

She had asked Luke hesitantly once why his parents stayed together when they were so obviously not happy. His mouth had tightened, and he had told her bitterly, 'My mother loves him...'

Then she had been too young and naïve to know exactly what that meant... what a terrible burden such a love must be both to his mother and to Luke.

Now, with clearer, distant vision, she could see how Luke had worked savagely to maintain the fiction of his parents' marital happiness in order to protect his mother, and she also recognised what a tremendous burden that must have been for him.

No child should bear the burden of being responsible for its parents' happiness... She sighed, angry with herself for permitting herself to feel sympathy for him.

Eleanor's dinner party was due to commence at half-past eight, but Jenneth had agreed to be there earlier to give her friend a hand.

At half-past six she was ready to leave, wearing a new dress Eleanor had persuaded her to buy in a moment of madness when she had been shopping for an outfit for Louise's wedding. The silky black and white fabric had a softly bloused top with cap sleeves that revealed the slenderness of her arms, tanned now from her day in the garden. It had a neat boat-shaped neck, demure, so she had thought, not recognising the allure of the way the fabric revealed the delicacy of her collarbone and the feminine arch of her throat.

The skirt was a fan of swirling knife pleats flaring out at hip-level and emphasised by the provocatively twenties-style way the dress narrowed above the pleats, the fabric tying at the waist in a soft floppy bow.

Angelica was playing dominoes with the twins when Jenneth went downstairs. Her eyes opened wide in pleased appreciation as she studied Jenneth's appearance, and she said wistfully, 'I wish you were my real mummy, Jenneth, and not just my pretend one.' And then she pressed herself close to Jenneth, burying her face in her skirt, while the twins exchanged glances that Jenneth didn't see.

Neither did she see Luke walking into the room, his suit jacket off, his shirt unbuttoned at the throat.

It was only the sharpness of the way he spoke to Angelica, telling her that Jenneth was going out and that she was not to spoil her dress, that alerted Jenneth to his presence, and as she felt Angelica's tension she hugged her protectively, looking frigidly at Luke for his unnecessary sharpness, and then said softly into Angelica's hair, 'Don't worry, love... you haven't done any damage.'

She gave Luke another acid look, her eyes narrowing a little as she recognised the tiredness in his eyes. His shirt-sleeves were rolled up, exposing powerful tanned forearms, and along his jaw she could see the beginnings of a day's growth of beard... Her head lurched suddenly and betrayingly and, across the five or six feet that separated them, she was overpoweringly and acutely aware of the hot male scent of his skin.

Disengaging herself from Angelica, and dropping a quick kiss on her head, she said quickly, 'I must go...' Then, snatching up her white linen jacket and her handbag, she hurried to the door, pausing only to remind the twins of their responsibilities toward Angelica.

'Don't worry.' Nick grinned at her. 'We'll make sure she's in bed for eight.' He laughed as Angelica scowled at him, ruffling her hair and then picking her up, making her shriek with mingled outrage and excitement.

Eleanor, as Jenneth already knew, was a superb hostess, skilled not only at providing the kind of meal that made her guests envy her her domestic abilities, but also at assembling a blending of guests that kept the conversation and the adrenalin flowing.

'Who's coming tonight?' Jenneth asked her, as they worked together putting the final touches to the elegant mahogany dining-table.

'The Allisons...' Eleanor told her, mentioning a couple who were old friends, and who knew Jenneth quite well. 'Adrian Barbary...' She saw the look Jenneth gave her and grinned unrepentantly. 'I promise you I am not matchmaking...' And then, when Jenneth gave her a withering look, she complained, 'Can I help it if the poor man has a crush on you?'

She laughed as Jenneth went faintly pink, and amended with another grin, 'Actually I didn't invite him for your benefit. I know I'd be wasting my time, but I can't help feeling sorry for him. He's been so alone since his mother died...'

Jenneth gave her another withering look, while Eleanor avoided her eyes, and delicately licked some salmon mousse off her finger.

'Just testing it,' she explained, putting the empty bowl into the dishwasher. 'Mmm . . . who else? Bill and Mary Seddons . . .' She pulled a face. 'Mary rang me this morning and asked me if they could bring someone with them . . . a colleague of Bill's, apparently . . .'

Bill Seddons was a member of the local council, and Jenneth liked both Bill and Mary, his wife.

'How are things going at home?' Eleanor suddenly asked Jenneth quietly, watching with shrewd affection as Jenneth ducked her head so that her hair swung across her jawline, obscuring her expression.

'Not very well,' she admitted, breaking off as the doorbell rang.

While Eleanor went to answer it, Jenneth walked out into the pretty conservatory that Eleanor had had added to the house after her husband's death. Its two sets of double doors were both open, creating a welcome waft of air. Beyond the conservatory was a well-designed paved sitting area with pathways leading off it into the garden. Huge Ali Baba-shape jars filled with masses of tumbling plants broke up the empty space, and the old-fashioned bourbon roses growing on the house wall filled the air with their rich scent as Jenneth walked outside.

She heard footsteps coming through the conservatory, and Adrian Barbary's voice mingling with that of Eleanor and the Allisons, and, putting as bright a smile as she could on her face, she turned round and went to join the others.

Ten minutes later, when the doorbell went again just as Eleanor was pouring people's drinks, she exclaimed ruefully, 'It's at times like these that I most miss having a resident man. Would you finish these for me while I go and let the others in?' she asked Jenneth.

Jenneth was just pouring herself a glass of the white wine cooler that was one of Eleanor's specialities when Eleanor returned with Bill and Mary and their visitor.

Jenneth turned round to greet them, the smile dying on her face, to be replaced by a shocked disbelief as she saw Luke standing easily with Bill and Mary, responding to Eleanor's greeting.

He hadn't seen her, or so she thought, but suddenly he turned his head and was looking directly at her, and Eleanor, for once oblivious to the undercurrent running between them, started to introduce him to Jenneth.

It was Luke who stopped her, saying easily, 'Jenneth and I already know one another... In fact,' he added, giving the assembled group a smile that made Jenneth clench her fists in fierce resentment, 'Jenneth is at present my landlady...'

There was a small, confused silence of the kind that occurs when good manners prevent people from giving rein to their real feelings; in this case, quite obviously, feelings of acute astonishment, except in the case of Adrian, who glowered suspiciously at Luke and then said unwisely, 'Jenneth, surely this isn't true?'

Adrian was very much the product of his mother's extremely narrow-minded upbringing and, in addition to her resentment against Luke, Jenneth was equally angry at Adrian's obvious disapproval.

It was left to her to explain through tightly clenched teeth, 'Luke is an . . . an old family friend. He and his daughter are staying with us until he finds a suitable house . . .'

Everyone apart from Eleanor accepted her statement at face value.

The Allisons, unwittingly protecting her, were questioning Luke about his new appointment, and Eleanor, taking pity on her friend's white face and tense expression, invited her to join her in the kitchen to make a final check on the meal.

Informality being the theme of the evening, none of the guests objected to being left to their own devices, but Jenneth was conscious of the sharp, shrewd look Luke gave her as she made her escape.

'So that's him!' Eleanor exclaimed once they were in the kitchen. She saw Jenneth's face and added calmly, 'No, I promise you I had no idea who he was; Bill and Mary simply asked if they could bring a colleague of Bill's, and I agreed . . .'

Jenneth felt a little of the tension ease from her aching muscles.

'I've been so on edge since Luke appeared that I think I'm becoming paranoid,' she said shakily.

Eleanor looked at her for a moment, and then said seriously, 'Well, at the risk of making you even more paranoid, I must say that your Luke seems a touch proprietorial towards you for a man who threw you over eight years ago to marry someone else.'

Jenneth stared at her.

'How can you say that?' she demanded. 'You've only seen him for about five minutes . . .'

'Plenty long enough to interpret the body language,' Eleanor assured her, 'and believe me, he

was giving off quite definite hands-off signals in
Adrian's direction...'

Jenneth wasn't listening to her. Now that the
shock of Luke's arrival was beginning to wear off,
a new hazard was tormenting her.

'I'm supposed to be spending the evening on a
heavy date,' she groaned.

'Well if he questions you about it, tell him you
changed your mind,' said Eleanor calmly.

Jenneth thought her friend was taking a rather
frivolous attitude to her problems, but Eleanor had
seen the determined, possessive way Luke had
looked at Jenneth when she wasn't aware of his
scrutiny, and she was by no means convinced that
he was anywhere near as indifferent to her as
Jenneth appeared to think.

Dinner was the kind of ordeal that Jenneth had
believed only existed in television plays.

When Luke had tired of subtly cross-examining
Adrian, and laid bare the paucity of Jenneth's relationship with the other man, he turned his attention to Jenneth herself, saying with deceptive
easiness, 'I must say it was quite a surprise to see
you here this evening, Jen...I thought you had a
dinner date *à deux*...'

Jenneth stared at him, knowing that her skin was
turning hot with embarrassment and misery, her
mind so blank that she couldn't think of a single
thing to say, and then to her surprise Eleanor came
to her rescue, saying lightly, 'She did, but I begged
her to cancel it and help me out with this dinner
party...'

Luke's eyebrows climbed queryingly. 'Friendship,
indeed. There aren't many women who would

cancel an evening with their current man to spend it helping out a friend...'

Jenneth was hot with embarrassment and anger. The other five dinner guests were looking at her with varying degrees of curiosity, no doubt wondering who this mythical man was, she reflected bitterly.

Once again, Eleanor rescued her, saying crisply, 'You're out of date, I'm afraid. These days modern women place much more value on their friendships.'

After dinner, escaping into the relative solitude of the garden, Jenneth wondered dismally how quickly she could escape. At least there was no need now for her to stay out late to maintain the fiction that she was with her lover.

Eleanor's garden was her pride and joy, designed after the style of Gertrude Jekyll, and, as Jenneth plucked restlessly at the petal of a white rose in a manner that would have horrified her hostess, she was oblivious to anyone else's presence until Luke said quietly to her, 'What a creature of constant surprises you are, Jenneth—giving up so many precious hours with your lover to help Eleanor. Where is he, by the way?' he asked blandly.

Jenneth bit into her bottom lip. Why was he persisting in torturing her like this? It was obvious that he knew she had been lying to him.

Furious with him and with herself for allowing him to goad her into such a senseless and humiliating situation, she swung round, dislodging a shower of the pale petals and releasing their musky, provocative scent into the air, her voice low and rough with emotion.

'All right, Luke... I admit it: I lied to you. There is no lover...' She turned her back on him, staring out into the velvet dusk of the garden with fixed concentration, willing him to go away as she demanded in a choked voice, 'Satisfied? You've marked me as your quarry...hunted me down...trapped me...' She turned round, her head tilting proudly as she glared bitterly at him, pride making her rise above the agony of her embarrassment. 'And now, if you'll excuse me...'

He stepped to one side to let her pass, watching her go with a half-brooding, half-wry weariness, muttering to himself with derisive self-contempt once she was out of sight, 'Great...you handled that really well, chum.' He bent down and scooped up a handful of the petals Jenneth had displaced, crushing them in his fist so that their intoxicating scent was immediately released as it had been when they'd fallen.

'Satisfied...' He grimaced to himself as he tasted the word, and wondered if Jenneth knew what a powerful weapon she held against him; then, discarding the rose petals, he walked slowly back to the house.

Eleanor found Jenneth in the kitchen, vigorously attacking what was left of the washing-up. She stood watching her for a few minutes before she said drily, 'That's quite some effect he has on you...'

'He's deliberately trying to torment me!' Jenneth exploded without turning round, her voice almost savage with all that she was feeling. 'Well, I've told him the truth,' she said crossly, finishing the glass of white wine cooler she had poured herself on her way in from the garden. Her confrontation with Luke had left her feeling hot and bothered, and the wine cooler was deliciously refreshing.

'That's about the fourth of those you've had,' Eleanor reminded her. 'Plus the Bordeaux with dinner.'

The Bordeaux had been excellent and had come from the small cellar Eleanor's husband had laid down. Wine had been one of his passions, and Eleanor admitted ruefully that she felt slightly guilty every time she opened one of his cherished bottles.

Recklessly Jenneth told her, 'I don't care. In fact, I'll have another glass...'

She half expected Eleanor to stop her, but as she turned aside to reach into the fridge for a fresh jug she thought she heard Eleanor uttering something about 'being over the limit now, anyway', although it wasn't until later that the remark sank in. At the moment, Jenneth, normally so abstemious when it came to any form of alcohol—having discovered the hard way as a teenager that she had a remarkably weak head where drink was concerned—was so worked up about Luke's almost demonical ability to reduce her to grovelling humiliation that she hadn't room to worry about anything else.

'Can you help me carry the iced coffees through?' Eleanor asked doubtfully, eyeing her friend's troubled face.

'Of course,' Jenneth assured her, watching as Eleanor deftly assembled glasses and a tall jug of the pale brown liquid which Jenneth already knew contained Eleanor's home-made ice-cream and some of her best brandy.

Later, sitting in the conservatory among the plants which were Eleanor's pride and joy while the warm evening air, heavy with scents from the garden, wafted in through the open doors, Jenneth justified her second glass of the delicious and potent coffee with the explanation that the heat was making her thirsty.

'Something, or rather someone, is definitely having an extremely unusual effect on you,' remarked Eleanor to her *sotto voce* as she walked past her. She wondered if Jenneth realised yet that she was going to have to stay the night. She was certainly in no fit state to drive.

When Jenneth enthusiastically accepted the liqueur she was offering, Eleanor intercepted the sharp, frowning look Luke sent her. Without causing any disturbance, he had somehow managed to extricate himself from his conversation with Bill and Mary, and was now sitting where he could watch Jenneth.

Refusing her friend's offer to help her collect the empty glasses with a grim smile at the potential fate of her crystal, she wondered with a little smile of sympathy how Jenneth was going to feel in the morning. Eleanor had never seen her drink more than one glass of wine at the most before.

At one o'clock, when Bill and Mary started making leaving noises, the Allisons and Adrian joined in. Jenneth tried to stand up and follow the general exodus through the house to the front door, but discovered that the tiled floor of the conservatory seemed to have become fluid and unstable. Having frowned reprovingly at it for several seconds and still not been able to make it remain solid, she sank back into her cane chair, a puzzled frown furrowing her forehead.

'A wise decision,' a familiar voice murmured against her ear, and she whirled round accusingly, glowering at Luke.

'Why don't you go away?' she suggested crossly, and sent him an even crosser glower when instead of moving he grinned at her and hunkered down beside her so that their eyes were almost on a level.

'You know, I don't think I've seen you pout like that since you were ten years old,' he told her.

'I'm *not* pouting.' Jenneth denied, and then added in a small, uncertain voice, 'I wish you would go away. You're making me feel dizzy and funny inside...'

Her eyes betrayed far more than she knew.

'Jenneth...' There was something in Luke's voice, some strong, sensual current, so intense that it broke through her alcoholic daze and made her breath catch in a sharp surge of awareness.

'Jenneth, I think I'd better take you up to my spare room...'

Neither of them had heard Eleanor come in, and Jenneth turned her head so abruptly that the dizziness came back and increased.

'I'll take Jenneth home,' she heard Luke saying, and through the mind-numbing influence of the wine she retained enough sense of self-preservation to say huskily,

'No... I can drive myself home...' Her eyes drew together in a puzzled frown as both Eleanor and Luke said fiercely together, 'No!'

Ignoring Jenneth's incoherent protests, Luke turned to Eleanor and assured her quietly, 'I promise you she'll be perfectly safe with me...'

'I'm sure she will,' agreed Eleanor drily. 'But will I be equally safe when she realises what I let her do?'

Luke laughed. 'We'll come and collect her car in the morning, if that's OK...' he said, in a way that made it perfectly plain to Eleanor that, if necessary, he was perfectly capable of virtually kidnapping Jenneth and taking her home.

'She doesn't normally drink very much at all,' Eleanor felt bound to say in her friend's defence.

Luke's smile vanished, his expression oddly vulnerable and haunted.

'No... I know,' he said quietly, and then he was bending over Jenneth, saying firmly, 'Come on, Jen, time to leave...'

To Eleanor's wry amusement her friend got uncertainly to her feet, and allowed Luke to guide her slowly towards the door.

CHAPTER SEVEN

'COME on, Jen...we're home now.'

Home...how lovely that word sounded, especially when spoken by that deep male voice that made her toes curl a little just to hear it.

Even so, she was deliciously comfortable where she was...warm and safe, breathing in a familiar man scent that made her want to stay where she was.

'Come on, Jen. There are two ways we can do this: either you get out of the car under your own steam and walk, or I carry you...'

The voice came from her other side now and cool air was wafting over her, forcing her to open her eyes. She did so reluctantly, frowning as she realised distantly that she was sitting in an unfamiliar car.

With its unfamiliarity came fine tendrils of apprehension which made her turn her head still further, until her gaze encountered that of the man watching her.

Relief filled her. It was Luke, and there was no reason for her to be afraid...no reason at all.

Instinctively she raised her arms toward him and said sleepily, 'Carry me, Luke...'

An odd, indefinable expression crossed his face, but she was too bemused to translate it, only giving a blissful sigh as he complied with her request and lifted her out of the car.

Instinctively she snuggled against him, her arms going around him as she closed her eyes and wished a little crossly that she didn't feel quite so dizzy.

Luke had to put her down to unlock the front door, and he was thankful to discover once he had got her inside that the house was in silence. The last thing he wanted to face was the twins' accusing faces when they saw the state of their sister. He felt guilty enough already, without them adding to that burden.

As he walked across the hall, Jenneth murmured something about wanting a drink. He tightened his hold on her grimly and went straight upstairs, glad of the relative lightness of the summer night so that he didn't have to switch on any lights and wake the twins.

He knew which was Jenneth's room; the door was already half open, but he was careful to close it gently behind him as he carried her over to her bed.

He put her on it gently, sighing faintly as he looked down into her face. Without the guard she wore whenever he was around, she looked so young. Hardly any older than she had looked at twenty-one. Her eyes were closed, a silky strand of hair brushing across her face. He reached out to remove it, the breath locking in his chest as he felt the never truly forgotten warm silkiness of her skin beneath his fingertips. How was it that the human senses could remember and react to one specific other human being's skin so intensely? As he traced her jawbone, her eyelashes fluttered.

She was still fully dressed and, while instinct warned him to leave her as she was, concern made him hesitate, knowing that she was almost bound to oversleep in the morning, and that her brothers, curious as to her whereabouts, were equally bound to invade her bedroom.

Knowing how sensitive she was, he could equally well imagine how much she would hate them finding her still fully dressed, obviously recovering from the effect of too much to drink.

He moved her gently, turning her over, reaching for her zip, and then stopped again.

Equally, and probably far more intensely, she would hate the thought of him undressing her, no matter how altruistic his motives.

As he hesitated, weighing the problem, she stirred and muttered something in her sleep, and, telling himself firmly that he was acting in her best interests, he found the zipper tag and eased it down swiftly.

No one could go through the early years of medical training without learning how to remove clothes with speed and efficiency, and he discovered that he had not entirely lost that skill. He hesitated about removing her bra, and then compromised by removing that article of clothing, but leaving her with the doubtful modesty of her briefs, wondering with wry self-irony why it was that this same brief article of clothing he felt sure he had seen in a pile of clean washing Jenneth had brought in from the garden, and which had then merely been a scrap of silky fabric, should suddenly have been transformed into a garment of such allure and temptation when adorning Jenneth's lissomly feminine body. As he sat up, she rolled over on to her stomach, exposing the delicate curve of her spine. He traced its descent visually, noting the

narrowness of her waist and the tender round-
edness of her bottom. She had surprisingly long
legs ... long and slim, with tiny, delicate ankles and
pretty pink feet.

He drew a deep breath as he realised what was
happening to him, and then another ... so much for
clinical detachment, he reflected ruefully, starting
to move away from the bed, automatically picking
up Jenneth's clothes.

Perhaps because the removal of his weight from
the mattress disturbed her, or perhaps because she
was only sleeping lightly, his withdrawal woke her,
her eyes opening and focusing on him before he
could move.

Jenneth blinked, and then blinked again, and
then said frowningly, 'You're real ... but you can't
be ... you're supposed to be part of my dream.' She
pinched her arm and scowled malevolently at her
soft flesh.

Perhaps unwisely, Luke moved back towards the
bed, dropping her clothes on to a chair.

'Jenneth, go back to sleep,' he told her. 'It's late,
and in the morning ...'

'In the morning you'll be gone,' Jenneth finished tightly. 'Just like all the other mornings.' She
focused on him again, her eyes huge and brilliant
with unshed tears.

'Don't leave me, Luke,' she pleaded, stretching
her arms out to him. 'Don't leave me this
time ... stay with me, please ...'

There were a hundred things he ought to say,
calm, reasoned explanations of why he couldn't
possibly do what she was suggesting, of how she
was going to feel in the morning if by some

mischance she should remember what she was saying to him now in her tipsy, inhibition-free state.

He had a responsibility towards her, never mind to himself, which was telling him loudly and clearly to ignore the pleading look in her eyes, and to walk away from her bed as quickly and quietly as he could.

But between him and that responsibility stood the spectre that had haunted him for eight years, the spectre of a young woman too hurt and too proud to let him see what he was doing to her, and in the shadows of Jenneth's eyes he saw now the ghost of that young girl, and he took one step towards the bed and then another.

Jenneth watched him with huge, dream-darkened eyes, and when he got closer she silently opened her arms to him, her body trembling between two pinnacles of emotion.

She had had this dream so often, but this was the first time it had been so real... Real enough for it to actually hurt when she pinched herself... Real enough for her to smell the scent of roses through her open bedroom window and to hear the uneven harshness of Luke's breathing.

He caught hold of her hands, turning them gently palms-uppermost as he prevented her from coming any closer. She frowned in confusion. This wasn't part of the dream. In the dream, he always welcomed her into his arms, touching her, kissing her with an urgency that made her own flesh catch fire.

He was speaking to her too, soft, low-spoken words she had to strain to catch, something about regrets and this not being the time or the place.

He bent his head and touched his mouth to the pulse in her wrist, a tender, almost asexual, caress that made her body prickle with despair.

He released her quickly and moved away, heading for the door. Jenneth watched him go in confused despair. It was never normally like this . . . normally—normally he took her in his arms and held her against the fierce heat of his male flesh, whispering to her how much he ached for her . . . how much he needed her.

She got out of bed, calling out his name in a husky, anguished voice.

As she stood up, the room swung dizzily around her. Luke turned, saw her sway unsteadily and turned back to the bed, catching hold of her to support her.

As she felt the harshness of fabric against her own nakedness where there should only have been the smooth hardness of answering male flesh, Jenneth frowned.

'It's all right, Jenneth,' Luke told her, sensing her confusion, and then, totally unable to stop himself, he bent his head and kissed her mouth gently, smiling a little against her lips as he touched them with his tongue and tasted the wine sweetness of them.

It should have stopped there. He fully intended that it *would* stop there, but she moved, and somehow the hand that had been resting supportingly against her back was now pressing against the softness of her breast, and beneath his mouth her lips parted on a soft gasp of reaction.

'Hell, Jenneth, don't do this to me,' he muttered against her mouth, knowing that he couldn't . . . that he dared not allow himself to make love to her while she was in what amounted to an alcoholic daze, and yet unbearably tempted to take advantage of what the fates were offering him; not for the greedy possession of her body, but for the opportunity it afforded him to manoeuvre her into the position he wanted.

Her body moved innocently and accommodatingly against his, her mouth soft and inviting, and then suddenly no longer passive but actively inciting as she nibbled tormentingly at his bottom lip, flicking her tongue teasingly over the closed line of his mouth, while the unintentionally provocative movement of her body against his own made him achingly aware of the soft swell of her breasts, and the way her hips seemed to curve so naturally into his hands that it was the hardest thing in the world not to hold her and lift her so that he could press the grinding ache of his own arousal into her softness.

Her mouth teased and seduced, and then suddenly pouted centimetres away from his ear as she complained crossly, 'This isn't like my dream at all. You aren't doing any of the things I want you to do...'

And, knowing he was likely to damn himself for eternity, but totally unable to stop himself, he heard himself asking in a slow, strained voice, 'What do you want me to do, Jenneth?'

For a moment he thought she had realised what was happening. She drew back from him and he let her go, half of him hoping that she had returned to full awareness, the other half... Well, he preferred not to dwell on how the other half felt.

But she frowned and seemed not to be looking at him but gazing instead into the darkness, and he realised that she still had no idea that this was reality and not her dream. He knew he ought to leave, but the temptation to stay, after so many long years of being without her, of being forced to live a lie...of being forced to...

She gave him a look that was half bold and half shy, and then said huskily, 'You know...'

He shook his head.

'No...I don't. You'll have to tell me...or show me,' he added fatally.

Jenneth looked owlishly at him. Show him...well, it seemed a reasonable suggestion, so she went up to him and said solemnly, 'Well, first you have to kiss me. Properly, I mean.' Shadows darkened her eyes, as she added quietly, 'You hardly ever did...not really...'

So she had known that. He had often wondered...but he had promised her parents he would not violate their trust in him, and they had not wanted their daughter rushed into a sexual relationship before she was ready.

Now, looking down into the sad darkness of her eyes, he found himself saying 'Like this, you mean?' And then he lowered his mouth to hers, hesitating for half a second while he stroked her lips tenderly with his thumb and felt them quiver betrayingly beneath the delicate abrasion.

They were still trembling when he covered them with his mouth. He had told himself that there was no real danger...that all the years of exercising restraint and control would make it impossible for him to lose his head...but he had forgotten that

Jenneth was a woman now and not a girl, and the sensation of holding her, touching her, tasting her, engulfed him so totally and so rapidly that it was like standing in the path of an avalanche.

Between kisses, while she removed his shirt so that she could have the access to his chest that she demanded, he asked her what else it was she wanted him to do, and received in reply a soft whisper that made him fit his palms around her breasts until the frantic pounding of her heart made him release her and carry her over to the bed, sitting her on its edge before he dropped to his knees in front of her and covered their softness again, this time slowly drawing his hand away as he kissed the delicate flesh with a tenderness that gave way to aching desire when he lifted his head and saw the intoxicating blend of awe and need in Jenneth's eyes.

'And this?' he demanded rawly, against her skin. 'Do you want me to do this, Jenneth?'

The low cry she gave as he drew gently on the hard tip of her breast made his body shudder and the sweat spring out of his pores. Against his tongue her nipple felt provocatively hot and tight, and he drew on it fiercely so that it throbbed eagerly. Jenneth, her body arched by the savage spasm of pleasure that arced from her breast to her womb, dug her nails into his shoulders and gave a softly erotic moan.

'Shush...' Luke cautioned her thickly. 'You mustn't make any noise, not this time...' But Jenneth wasn't really listening. She was shivering from head to foot with reaction, a raw, uncontrollable ache that pulsed inside her, and she turned towards him, her eyes huge and blind with a shocked arousal that gave away the extent of her reaction to him.

'Jenneth ...' He said her name on a husky groan, thinking of all the ways he wanted to please her and all the reasons why he must not.

It would be so easy to take her now, to lay her down and to silence the soft, exciting little noises she would make.

While he trembled between need and necessity... holding her shivering body against the warmth of his own, so that her breasts were pressed against the hardness of his naked chest, her face tucked into the angle of his throat ... the bedroom door suddenly opened and Angelica walked in, saying crossly, 'Jenneth, I can't find my daddy, and I've got a tummy ache...'

And then she stopped dead and stared from her father to Jenneth, her eyes going round with surprise.

'Daddy, why are you cuddling Jenneth?' she asked him suspiciously.

Jenneth, who had been nuzzling his skin, suddenly realised that they weren't alone, and raised her head to look at Angelica, confusion and alcohol still dimming her perceptions.

'Jenneth hasn't got any clothes on,' Angelica added accusingly, and Luke, knowing that there was no way he was ever going to be able to silence the inquisitive child, gave up battling against fate and took the opportunity he was being handed, saying calmly to her,

'Angelica, Jenneth and I are going to get married...'

Jenneth heard him and stared at him. Several confusing events were taking place in her dream; odd, unexpected events that were causing her stomach to flutter nervously.

'Does that mean that Jenneth will be my real mummy instead of a pretend?' Angelica asked complacently.

When Luke nodded, she gave a whoop of delight, watching as Luke deftly eased Jenneth beneath the bedclothes and tugged the covers up around her, ignoring her slurred protests that this wasn't like any of her dreams at all and saying firmly to Angelica, 'Jenneth needs to go to sleep, and I want to know what you've eaten to give you a tummy ache, my girl.'

Jenneth woke up reluctantly with an appalling taste in her mouth, and a pounding headache that refused to allow her to lift her head off the pillow.

To make matters worse, splinteringly bright sunlight was pouring in through her bedroom window, and as she groaned and tried to close her eyes against it she heard Angelica's excited piping voice exclaiming, 'Jenneth, please wake up! I want to talk to you about when you're my real mummy...'

A disjointed series of half-remembered events crashed through her stunned brain, and Jenneth sat bolt upright in bed, ignoring the queasy protests of her head and stomach until she realised that she was virtually naked.

Subsiding equally speedily beneath the bedclothes, she shuddered sickly and prayed that none of her dreadfully disturbing memories of last night had any bearing on reality.

She focused unhappily on Angelica, and was just about to remind her that it was unlikely that she would ever become her mother when her bedroom door opened and Luke walked in, saying firmly, 'Angelica, I told you that you weren't to disturb Jenneth...'

'But she's awake now,' Angelica protested, and the sinking sensation in the pit of her stomach increased as Jenneth realised that she simply could not lie there with her eyes closed for the rest of her life, cravenly wishing that Luke would go away.

She opened them briefly and groaned.

'Classic hangover symptom,' she heard Luke saying cheerfully. 'Not to worry... We'll soon have you feeling more human.'

'Well...how's the bride-to-be feeling this morning?' Nick asked from the doorway, and while Jenneth looked wildly from her brother's amused face to Luke's unreadable one, certain horrid convictions began to spring up in her mind with the rapidity and hardiness of the dragon's teeth of legend.

'I was the first to know,' said Angelica importantly. ''Cos I came in and found Daddy kissing you,' she told Jenneth, adding with an innocence that at any other time Jenneth might have found touching, but which right now made her shudder with self-revulsion, 'and you didn't have any clothes on and Daddy wasn't wearing his shirt...'

Jenneth gave a low moan, and for once in her life abandoned her fierce, stoical pride and pulled the bedclothes up over her head, saying thickly, 'Go away, all of you...'

She heard Nick laugh, and then Kit say, 'Too late now, sis... I'm afraid you're going to have to make an honest man of him. Luke's explained everything to us,' he added gravely.

What had Luke explained to them? Jenneth wondered bitterly. And why on earth had he told Angelica she was going to be her mother?

She dropped the sheet and pushed it away from her face, looking at her brothers suspiciously.

'You and Luke getting married...' Kit marvelled.

As she opened her mouth to tell her brother just how wrong he was, Luke said casually, 'I thought it best to give them our good news, darling, especially in view of the fact that Angelica beat me to the breakfast-table and had already regaled your brothers with her description of how she had interrupted us last night...'

There were a dozen things she ought to say, but none of them seemed to fit around her tongue. Her head was pounding fit to burst, and the last thing she felt capable of coping with was explaining to the twins that although Angelica had apparently found her as near as damn it naked in Luke's embrace, that did not mean that there was any reason for Luke to marry her. She looked at Luke, her expression conveying anger, pain and confusion, her mouth dry and tasting bitter, and she realised that Luke had no intention of helping her to explain the truth.

One hand on Angelica's shoulder, he smiled at Jenneth and he said calmly, 'A cold shower, some breakfast and a gentle walk around the garden and you'll feel much better... However, seeing as this appears to be your first hangover, I think we'll cosset you a little and allow you a cup of tea first...'

And then he marshalled everyone out of her room, leaving her to brood miserably on the idiocy of her own behaviour, while her skin alternately burned and chilled as her memory provided vivid and very unwanted footage of just what she had said and done, and of how Luke had cruelly let her humiliate herself.

A cup of tea... She took advantage of her momentary reprieve to walk unsteadily into her bathroom and to lock the door firmly behind her while she tried to understand why Luke was allowing this farce of their getting married to continue.

Surely there must have been an easier way of explaining the situation? Like what? her conscience derided. Like telling everyone you were seducing him?

She shuddered sickly and leaned against the bathroom door, letting tears of anger and humiliation slide down her face. How could she have done it? How could she have betrayed herself to that extent?

And how *could* Luke have let her? Why on earth hadn't he stopped her? He *must* have realised... *must* have known—*must* surely have been able to forestall her... So why hadn't he done so?

CHAPTER EIGHT

EVEN with the generous amount of space provided by a large, rambling Victorian house and its equally large and rambling garden, it was remarkably difficult to avoid any other human contact, Jenneth reflected bitterly as she took refuge in her studio, for the first time in her life stooping to what she privately considered to be the cowardly subterfuge of putting a 'Keep out - work in progress' sign that the twins had once bought her as a Christmas present on her studio door.

As she hung it there, nervously glancing over her shoulder in case either one of the twins or Angelica had managed to track her down, she inwardly railed impotently against Luke, who surely was responsible for this whole fiasco.

Why on earth had he deemed it necessary to escort her to her bedroom in the first place...? Her hand left the worn oak door of the studio as though the wood had scorched her, ashamed colour firing her skin as she slunk back inside and closed the door, wishing it was as easy to close her mind against the horrid images of Luke picking her up and carrying her upstairs.

She made a small, despairing sound in her throat and shuddered.

How could she have been so stupid, especially when she knew she had no head for alcohol? She tried to remember anything she might have done or said during the dinner party that might cause her embarrassment, but the only thing that stuck in her mind was the shock of Luke's arrival.

It was his fault that she had had so much to drink. It had been because . . .

Because it had been the only way she had had of escaping from him, she acknowledged with self-irony. Some escape!

She still couldn't understand what quixotic motive had led him to announce that they were getting married. Unwillingly she remembered Angelica's almost incoherent joy, the way she had flung herself into her arms the moment she appeared downstairs, chattering excitedly about weddings and bridesmaids and having a real mother . . .

Even the twins had been pleased. No doubt they saw her marriage to Luke as a good way of offloading the responsibility of her on to another pair of male shoulders, she decided with unaccustomed bitterness.

She heard a car pull up outside the house and then its door slam, and curiosity drew her up to the window, too late to dodge out of sight when her visitor caught sight of her and waved enthusiastically.

Jenneth sighed. Meg Lawson was a chatterbox and almost as much of a gossip as Laura Gosford, but there was nothing malicious in her curiosity about the lives of people around her. She was well liked in the village, and worked tirelessly for several local charities.

Jenneth guessed that she was probably collecting for one of them now, and, knowing that she could hardly remain barricaded in her studio now that Meg had seen her, she reluctantly opened the door.

Meg beamed at her, pausing to catch her breath, and as Jenneth went towards her Luke and Angelica suddenly emerged from the house.

'There she is, Daddy,' Angelica crowed triumphantly, letting go of Luke's hand and darting across to Jenneth's side.

'I heard you had visitors,' Meg told Jenneth, her eyes darting from Jenneth to Angelica, and then across to Luke, who was strolling over to join them.

There was nothing Jenneth could do, other than stand there with a sickly smile pinned to her face.

Meg was asking Angelica her name. Jenneth took her attention off the little girl and her neighbour, unable to stop herself from watching Luke.

He gave her a faint smile; a compassionate smile, she might have thought in other circumstances.

'And Jenneth is going to be my new mummy, 'cos she and my Daddy are getting married...'

Jenneth stiffened as she heard Angelica proudly deliver this important statement, her eyes unwittingly imploring Luke for help as she registered the full measure of the disaster which had just occurred.

Meg was looking both pleased and excited, as well she might with such a juicy item of gossip to take home with her, Jenneth thought bitterly.

'Jenneth, my dear... how exciting! Have you known one another long?' she added.

It was Luke who answered her, not, as Jenneth had prayed, by refuting Angelica's statement, but by standing at Jenneth's side and putting one arm around her and the other round his daughter, so that the three of them were posed as a close-knit trio.

'Almost all our lives,' he replied easily, and then, turning to Jenneth, he gave her a slow, warm smile that made her eyes widen incredulously in disbelief that he should be able to manufacture so blatant and totally fictitious an expression of almost fatuous adoration.

And then, before Jenneth could stop him, he had reached for her hand and raised it to his mouth, kissing the softness of her palm, and then curling her fingers around it.

Her heart seemed to pound double-time, her body reacting to him so intensely and so quickly that her face flamed with the heat that washed through her.

'So romantic,' Meg sighed. 'When do you plan to marry?'

Again it was Luke who answered.

'Just as soon as it can be arranged,' he told her. 'In fact, Jenneth and I plan to call on the vicar tomorrow...'

'You'll be marrying here in the village? How lovely! Well, I mustn't keep you—you will be busy...'

And she was gone, almost running back to her car, before Jenneth could either deny Luke's monstrous lies or remind her that she hadn't explained the purpose of her visit.

Mindful of Angelica's presence, Jenneth said with as much control as she could muster, 'You realise that everything you've told her will be all round the village by teatime?'

Luke shrugged, giving her a lazy, teasing smile. 'Well, it saves putting a notice in the local paper... and now that I'm about to be a married man, one has to think of these small economies...'

Dear heaven, what was he trying to do to her? He was so relaxed about the whole thing... so... uncaring. No, *not* uncaring, she realised on a sharp, disbelieving stab of awareness. He was actually behaving as though he was pleased. As though... Her mind balked at the words forming in her brain. How could he *possibly* be pleased? He had rejected her... broken their engagement...

She turned away from him blindly, instinctively seeking the security of her studio, not seeing the wistful look Angelica gave her, nor Luke bending towards his daughter and saying calmly, 'Angie, you go back in the house for a few minutes. I want to talk to Jenneth...'

She didn't even realise he had followed her into her studio until she turned to close the door and saw him standing framed in it.

Her heart leapt and thudded frantically: the adrenalin of anger, and something else, something hopeless and unwanted; something that transported her back across the years to the tremulously eager girl she had once been, and fired her blood.

'How could you do that?' she demanded, shaking with the intensity of her own emotions. 'How could you stand there and deliberately tell her that we're getting married?'

'Because we are,' he responded calmly. And then, before she could speak, he added grimly, 'Did you really think we had any choice... after last night?'

It was like having an already painful sensitive area of flesh flicked with a whip, the pain instant and stingingly raw, so that she almost winced physically beneath it.

'That could have been explained.' She couldn't look at him. Her lips had gone very dry, and she licked at them nervously.

'Could it?' Luke demanded harshly. 'How?'

'I'd had too much to drink,' Jenneth protested despairingly.

'And weren't responsible for what you were doing? Is that really what you'd have preferred me to tell the twins?'

She flinched beneath the sarcasm in his voice, chewing miserably on her bottom lip.

'They're very protective of you, Jenneth,' he told her flatly. 'Very protective and very, very proud. Have you any idea what it would do to them to learn that their sister had so much to drink that...?'

'Don't!' she cried out in anguish, covering her face with her hands. 'Don't.'

She couldn't bear to look at him...hating him for seeing her like this with her defences down, her pride broken and trampled...hating herself for allowing him to see her like this. Not once, but twice...She shuddered, remembering how she had broken down when he ended their engagement, sick with the pain that pounded in her heart and the nausea that churned in her stomach, neither of them alcohol-induced, but caused by the tension that was gripping her mind and body.

'Do you really think I had any alternative?' Luke demanded witheringly. 'I have Angelica to think about, Jenneth. It isn't easy for a man alone to bring up a daughter, especially one as vulnerable and impressionable as mine. Like the twins, she's inclined to put you on a pedestal...'

'Me?' She dropped her hands staring at him in disbelief.

'Surely you knew that?' he derided her. 'I don't think she's spoken a single sentence that doesn't contain the words "Jenneth says..." since we got here.'

'And whose fault is that?' Jenneth demanded, resenting the additional burden of guilt he was making her carry. 'I didn't invite you to move in here.'

'No.' Luke agreed blandly, 'But the twins did, and in their way they're just as vulnerable as Angelica...'

He paused, watching her as the words sank in. He was right and Jenneth knew it; had he turned down the twins' invitation they would have felt rejected and hurt.

'Quite the amateur psychologist, aren't you?' she said bitterly.

His mouth twitched; the very fact that he could be amused when all she could feel was pain and despair incited her to demand fiercely, 'So what do you suggest we do now? We're going to have to tell them that we're not getting married...'

There was a long pause, during which for some reason the hairs on the back of her neck rose and prickled warningly.

'Not necessarily.' Luke said carefully at last. He walked past her towards the window and stood staring out at the garden. 'In fact, I think it would be a very good idea if we did get married...'

'What?' Jenneth couldn't believe her ears. 'What are you saying, Luke?' she demanded stiffly. 'You made it plain enough eight years ago that you didn't want me as your wife.'

'That was eight years ago.'

He turned round and looked at her, his face cold and remote, no suggestion to be read there that this was any kind of joke.

'Luke, I don't know what kind of game you're playing——' Jenneth began weakly.

'No game,' he interrupted her. 'You and I are going to be married, Jenneth . . . make no mistake about it.'

Going to be married . . . She blinked and looked disbelievingly at him, tensing as she saw what was in his eyes.

'You intended this to happen all along, didn't you?' she accused shakily. 'But why . . . why? You don't want *me* as your wife, even if Angelica wants me as her . . .' She blenched, her voice arrested as the truth exploded into her mind.

'Oh, dear heaven,' she said huskily. '*That's* why. You're marrying me because of Angelica . . . because Angelica wants a mother. Well, I won't do it, Luke——' she told him frantically, so deeply engrossed in the truth she had just perceived that she wasn't aware of the expression shadowing his face, turning it into a grimly resolute mask until he said curtly,

'You will, you know. You have no choice. Think, Jenneth,' he cautioned her. 'We've gone too far to turn back now. The whole village knows that I'm living here with you, and has probably drawn all manner of conclusions about the true nature of the relationship between us. In fact, when I was in the post office yesterday, buying a paper, I heard someone in the queue behind me whispering to her friend that I'd moved in with you. How long do you think it will be before the twins' friends start making pointed remarks about our relationship? They won't like that, will they? By your own example you've given them a moral code that may well be out of step with the time, but you know as well as I do that neither of them would react kindly to any outside suggestions that you and I are merely casual lovers.

'And then there's Angelica to think of. Already she's attached herself to you emotionally...' He looked at her and then said quietly, 'She needs you in her life, Jenneth.'

She looked back at him, hating him for what he was doing to her, aching to cry out to him, What about my needs? Don't I have the right to expect to marry a man who loves me...who wants me...not just as a mother for his daughter, but for myself?

She made one last desperate bid for freedom, saying frantically, 'I don't want to marry you, Luke. There's someone else...several someone elses, as a matter of fact——'

But he cut her off derisively, saying, 'Don't lie to me, Jenneth. You and I know that the reason any gossip about my being your lover might hurt the twins is because there *haven't* been any lovers...'

He paused for a moment, letting his words sink in, while Jenneth went sheet-white and swayed with shock. He reached out to help her but she fended him off, her eyes wild with shock and pain.

'I'd prefer not to imagine how much of the responsibility for that lies at my door, but my conscience won't let me,' he added quietly. 'Jenneth...'

Please don't let him touch me, her brain screamed, while her body froze into a pose of cringing terror. If he touches me now I'll die, she thought frantically, but even as he reached for her the door opened and Kit came in, grinning when he saw them.

'There you are. Louise has just been on the phone. I've told her the good news about you and Luke. She says you've got to come and speak to her immediately...'

It couldn't be happening, Jenneth thought sickly. It was all going to turn out to be a hideous but thankfully unreal nightmare. It had to be. The thought of having to marry Luke... of actually becoming his wife...

He touched her arm lightly and she flinched.

'Tell Louise that Jenneth will ring her back,' he told Kit quietly, and then, when Kit had gone, he said softly to her, 'It won't be so bad, Jenneth, I promise you.'

Before she could stop him, he took her in his arms, and held her as gently as though she was Angelica's age, rocking her soothingly in his arms as she shivered nauseously under the combined impact of shock and fear, telling her over and over again that she wasn't to worry and that everything would be all right.

After that, a numbing, weary acceptance seemed to engulf her, to the point where she accepted people's good wishes and questions about the wedding with a vague smile instead of the words of denial she ought to have been able to utter.

She couldn't even raise the energy to be frightened by the speed with which Luke wanted them to be married, balking only when he announced that they were to be married in church.

'Yes,' he had insisted fiercely, when she had tried to argue, overriding her protests with an intensity of emotion that surprised her; all the more so because she knew his first marriage had been conducted in a register office.

It was as though everyone close to her was involved in a conspiracy against her which made it impossible for them to see the truth; even Eleanor, who had thrown herself into preparations for the wedding with enthusiasm and *élan* was deaf to her protests that she couldn't marry Luke.

'You love him,' she had told her firmly, as though that in itself was enough, when Jenneth knew that it wasn't; and she was left with the feeling that the whole world was out of step with her and that nothing she might say or do would make any difference.

She tried to reason with Luke, but she hardly ever saw him. He had taken up his new position at the hospital and seemed to be working twenty hours out of every twenty-four.

Her work, once her solace, seemed to have turned traitor on her, and the day she discovered she was absent-mindedly painting Luke's features on to a mural commissioned by one of her clients, she had put down her brush and despairingly acknowledged that there was no way out and that she was trapped. Not so much by Luke, but by her own inability to hurt others, especially someone as young and vulnerable as Angelica.

Angelica, who was thrilled with the idea of Jenneth becoming her mother... Angelica, who talked non-stop about the wedding with such stars in her eyes that Jenneth couldn't bring herself to say the words that would destroy them... Angelica, who followed her as faithfully as her own shadow.

What stunned her the most was that no one, not even Louise, seemed surprised that she and Luke should be marrying. Louise's mother had rung her to tell her how thrilled they all were. They were all coming to the wedding, and Jenneth, who had not thought beyond wishing she could simply close her eyes and then open them to discover the whole thing was a nightmare, panicked until Eleanor told her calmly that she had everything under control and that all Jenneth had to do was to buy herself a wedding dress.

A wedding dress! Once she had dreamed of the dress she would wear to marry Luke. Now the mere thought turned her cold with distaste. Her rebellious heart demanded to know why it was necessary to go through this travesty... destroying something sacred and special, simply because Luke in his arrogance had decided she would make a good substitute mother for Angelica. Her equally rebellious tongue wanted to make the same demand of Luke himself, but she never seemed to get any time alone with him, much less enough to tell him all the reasons why it was impossible for them to marry.

Her thoughts turned to those humiliating moments when he had casually announced that he knew she hadn't any lovers. Too late now to resent that omission. She wondered uneasily just what sort of marriage Luke intended theirs to be, and then dismissed her apprehensions as idiotic. He felt no desire for her as a woman, that was obvious . . . and a relief.

If she had to marry him, she needed at least to retain some vestige of self-respect, and she knew there would be none if Luke chose to make love to her.

She had learned already that her self-control was no match for the feelings that bedevilled her when he touched her. She shuddered a little and tried to ignore the tide of panic rising inside her.

Only two more days. She hadn't bought a wedding dress. Eleanor had wheedled and cajoled, but she had stood firm. No wedding dress, no bridal finery, nothing.

'Then what will you get married in?' Eleanor had asked her, and she had shrugged uncaringly, and said bitterly, 'Sackcloth and ashes seem the most appropriate . . .'

Eleanor had ignored her . . . Just as everyone seemed to be ignoring her attempts to make them realise how little she wanted this marriage.

She and Luke were going to continue to live here in the house that had been her home since her parents' death. Luke was buying out the twins' share, and the money was being invested for them. At the same time he had told them both that they were always to consider the house their home, and had said it in such a way that Jenneth had felt tears sting her eyes in an acid pain that briefly penetrated the shocked miasma of misery she had wrapped round herself.

How, when he was so sensitive to the feelings of others, so concerned for them, could he possibly be so oblivious to hers? So deliberately and cruelly determined to ignore the need crying out in her to be set free from this hideous parody of all that a marriage should be?

How? Because her feelings didn't matter to him. He needed her to fill the empty space in Angelica's life. Jenneth had already witnessed his deep love for his daughter, witnessed it and envied it with a sharp bitterness that reflected the pain she had felt at losing him to Angelica's mother.

Angelica never mentioned her mother, and had no real memories of her, and Jenneth was surprised to discover that Luke rarely discussed her with his daughter. In some ways it was almost as though he didn't want Angelica to remember her... Because he didn't want to share his precious store of memories? That didn't seem to accord with the tender sensitivity she had seen him display.

To everyone apart from herself, she reminded herself bitterly.

Somewhere in the distance the telephone rang. She ignored its insistent call, wandering deeper into the garden, hiding herself from the world as she longed to be able to hide herself from Luke.

Escape...that was that she ached for...but there could be no escape other than in her dreams.

CHAPTER NINE

'WAKE up, Jenneth...it's a beautifully sunshiney day...and Aunt Eleanor has made you a special breakfast ...'

Wearily Jenneth opened her eyes, even now, on what she knew was going to be the worst day of her life, unable to deny Angelica's pleasure.

It was indeed a beautiful morning, the sky outside her window a perfect, unclouded blue, turning milky with heat haze in the distance.

Eleanor, who had stayed overnight, having spent the last few days performing feats of organisation that left Jenneth breathless, arrived with a breakfast tray boasting freshly squeezed orange juice, then slices of home-made brown toast, Angelica's favourite cereal, a bottle of champagne and a bowl of roses fresh from the garden, still damp with dew, their perfume rich and musky.

'The roses are from Daddy,' Angelica told her excitedly. 'We picked them together this morning 'cos he won't be able to see you until you're in church, and these are to remind you that he's thinking about you...'

Jenneth looked at them with fierce concentration, willing the stupid tears filling her eyes to go away.

Once before Luke had picked dew-fresh roses for her...the morning after he had proposed to her.

They too had arrived with a breakfast tray, brought up by her mother as a special treat. How different that day was...

'This is also from Luke.' Eleanor told her calmly, indicating the champagne and then chuckling. 'But you're only allowed one glass... I had the feeling that he was more than half inclined to bring it here himself,' she added wryly.

The look on her face said she suspected that, had he done so, it would have been because it was more than drinking champagne that he had in mind. What was it about weddings that made normally sensible people lose all their ability to reason? Jenneth wondered tiredly.

Eleanor knew that Luke didn't love her, and yet here she was looking all dewy-eyed and insinuating that Luke was an ardent, impatient lover, who had to be restrained from breaking into her bedroom and making passionate love to her.

A noise from outside caught her attention.

'What's that?' she demanded suspiciously.

'Oh, it's only the people erecting the marquee,' Eleanor told her blandly, for all the world as though the existence of the marquee was totally unworthy of comment, when Jenneth had told her that she did not want the kind of lavish reception Eleanor seemed to think necessary, and that she could see little point in celebrating an event that was in reality a desecration of all that it was meant to be.

'What marquee?' she exploded, leaping out of bed to rush to the window.

Outside on the lawn, the prettily striped marquee was already almost in place... She glared accusingly at Eleanor.

'People have to be fed,' Eleanor told her reasonably. 'Especially those who are travelling here.' Louise and George and her parents were coming, plus a couple of aged aunts who were Luke's as well as Louise's.

'Jenneth, what's wrong?' Angelica asked anxiously. 'You *do* like the marquee, don't you? I chose the colour...it's to match...' A tiny warning shake of the head from Eleanor caused her to flush and bite her lip as she fell silent, but Jenneth, overwhelmed with guilt, barely noticed.

'Of course I like it,' she lied with false heartiness. 'It's a wonderful surprise...'

Eleanor hid her amusement and her compassion by bustling about the bedroom, bullying Jenneth into drinking her juice and nibbling at a piece of toast.

The ceremony was taking place at three o'clock. Luke had spent the night at Eleanor's, in deference to the custom decreed that bride and groom should not spend the pre-wedding night under the same roof.

Downstairs, the doorbell rang.

'Oh, that will be the caterers,' announced Eleanor easily.

'Caterers?' Jenneth demanded suspiciously. 'What caterers?' But already it was too late. Eleanor was opening the door and hurrying downstairs.

Jenneth felt as though she had suddenly been caught up in the momentum of a fast-flowing river, carried with its currents whether she wanted to be or not.

The morning raced past with amazing speed. Virtually incarcerated in her room and kept there by Angelica, Jenneth fumed and fretted as downstairs the doorbell rang almost continuously and people came and went. When Eleanor had offered to organise things she had listlessly concurred, never dreaming that this would be the outcome.

Every time Jenneth had announced that she was getting up, Eleanor appeared as though by miracle to insist that she was to stay where she was. At twelve o'clock she appeared to announce that she would soon be sending someone up with a tray of lunch.

'Just as long as it isn't Luke,' said Jenneth bitterly, which for some reason seemed to convulse Angelica in gales of laughter.

At half-past twelve her bedroom opened and a familiar feminine voice called out gaily, 'What, still in bed? You're worse than I was.' And Jenneth's mouth fell open as Louise walked in, carrying not her lunch tray but an enormous cardboard box.

'Bet you were having kittens, thinking I might not make it,' she chuckled as she put the box down. 'But here we are, safe and sound.' She turned to Angelica, who was watching round-eyed, and said with a grin, 'Yours is in your room, sweetheart. Off you go, and Eleanor will help you with it, while Jenneth and I talk big girl secrets...'

Jenneth looked warily at her friend and then at the box, a sudden unwanted premonition gripping her.

'What's in it?' she demanded feebly.

Louise's eyebrows rose. 'Your dress, of course. I must say I was a bit startled when Luke rang up and told me what you wanted, but he explained

how busy you were. Did you get the mural finished, by the way?'

Mural... what mural?

Louise had her back to her as she knelt down to
remove the lid from the box.

'It should be a perfect fit. I know you're going
to love it. It's the most romantic thing I've *ever*
seen in my life...'

Jenneth stared at her best friend's back, while
the tears formed in her eyes and ran silently down
her face.

Alerted by some sixth sense, Louise turned round
and saw her. 'Hey, come on,' she said softly, going
over to her bed and putting her arms round her. 'I
know how you feel...all choked up and on the kind
of emotional see-saw you thought belonged only to
teenagers...'

Jenneth shook her head and managed to whisper
huskily, 'I don't want to marry Luke. I can't marry
him...'

To her dismay, Louise only laughed. 'Don't be
silly,' she chided her. 'Of course you want to marry
him. You love him...and he loves you...'

The words 'No, he doesn't' were on the tip of
her tongue when they both heard someone knock
briefly on her bedroom door.

'That will be our lunch,' Louise told her, getting
up and giving her a reassuring grin.

Two hours later, totally unable to believe what was
happening to her, Jenneth was walking down the
aisle with Nick on one side of her and Kit on the
other. She was wearing the impossibly beautiful
confection of silk and lace that Luke had appar-

ently chosen for her—although she suspected that only she knew that—and every pew in the small village church was crammed with well-wishers.

Behind her walked Angelica, her face incandescent with joy as she preened in her role as sole bridesmaid, the soft apricot colour of her dress perfect for her dark colouring.

There were flowers everywhere, huge bunches of artlessly natural colour and form, their scent filling the air.

The service was simple and achingly awesome. There was a moment, when Luke slipped the ring on to her finger, when Jenneth thought he might almost be shaking as much as she was herself, but it was gone so quickly that she had barely time to grasp at it, before it eluded her and was forgotten in the triumphal flood of organ music and the clear-tongued peal of the bells.

Events became a blur, the reception patterned with familiar faces and snatches of conversation.

She was a puppet, with no will of her own, her movements dictated by others. There were speeches, congratulations and laughter, hugs and kisses and, inevitably, tears, and then Eleanor was touching her arm and saying something about it being time for her to get changed.

Changed . . . she was already changed. Changed from herself into a stranger . . . Luke's wife. Odd how, when once she had ached for that mantle, it now chafed her tender skin and hurt her.

She allowed herself to be drawn upstairs. Someone had tidied up her bedroom. There was an unfamiliar suitcase on the bed, clothes neatly folded inside it. Eleanor went over to it and snapped down the lid.

'I don't think we've forgotten anything,' she told Jenneth, adding, 'Luke didn't say where he was taking you, but he told us what to pack...'

Louise was there, and Angelica. Louise told her to turn round while she unzipped her dress. Another one, a pretty slip of black and white silk, hung on the wardrobe door. Ignoring her protests, Louise unfastened the lace underwear she had worn beneath her dress and passed her instead a silk teddy of such a provocative cut and style that she said instinctively, 'I can't wear that...'

'Well, it's either that or nothing,' Louise told her mischievously, and because it was far easier to give in than to argue Jenneth unwillingly stepped into it, and then into the silk dress, and was hustled downstairs to where Luke was waiting for her, calm and somehow very intimidating.

As he led her towards the waiting car, she panicked and turned round, saying quickly, 'Angelica...the twins...'

'All taken care of,' Luke assured her. 'Eleanor's going to stay and keep an eye on them. We shan't be away very long...'

Jenneth gave a perceptible shudder. However long it was, it would be too long for her. Why was Luke doing this? Because his own pride demanded it? Because he didn't want people saying that he had only married her for Angelica's sake? Because it was expected of him?

She was too exhausted to care, only to resent that it had been necessary.

Somehow or other she was seated in the front passenger seat of the car, and they were moving off before she realised that she ought to have insisted on sitting in the back. At least that way she would have had some privacy... some precious time to try and come to terms with her new role in life.

She felt battered and exhausted. Too exhausted to ask where they were going, and, more importantly, why. If the wedding had been a farce, then how much more so was this cruelly unnecessary honeymoon?

When Luke stopped the car some miles outside the village, she sat apathetically, not questioning what he was doing until he released his seat-belt and from inside his jacket produced a familiar leather-covered box.

He heart lurched sickeningly as he flicked it open and she saw, lying on its bed of velvet, the engagement ring he had given her.

She had sent it back to him, unable to bear the sight of it. How could he have kept it and, even worse, produced it now, when he must surely realise what the sight of what she had once believed was a symbol of shared love and wanting would do to her?

Apparently he did not, because while she trembled and shuddered he took hold of her hand and said slowly, 'I think it's time this ring went back where it belongs, don't you, Jenneth?'

As he slid the ring over her knuckle, she wanted to claw and scream at him, to wrench it off and fling it away from her. The pain she felt inside was like a volcano erupting, but she knew that if she gave way to it now she would lose complete control of herself.

Her whole body went rigid with what she was feeling, and in a voice thick with loathing and bitterness, she said fiercely, 'Take it off...I won't wear it.'

Luke looked at her. A muscle twitched in his jaw.

'Jenneth,' he said quietly, but she ignored him and demanded again,

'Take it off.'

'No,' he told her curtly, turning away from her and restarting the car.

Impetuously, Jenneth tugged at it herself and found that for some reason she couldn't get it past her knuckle. The harder she tugged, the more swollen her knuckle became, and in the end, trembling with rage and resentment, she had to concede defeat. After that, neither of them spoke. The miles sped by, eaten up by the powerful engine of the Jaguar. They were travelling north-west, in the direction of the Yorkshire Dales.

It was early evening when Luke drove through a small, picturesque Dales village. On the other side of it he turned off the main road and along a narrow lane signposted 'Overdale House'.

The house was hidden from the lane by banks of rhododendrons. At the bottom of the valley below them snaked the silver ribbon of a river, and when the house eventually came into view its walls seemed to absorb the colour of the evening sun, so that the building was bathed in soft pink light.

It was an idyllic spot for a hotel, Jenneth acknowledged as Luke stopped the car. She guessed that the house had once been a private home—it

had that air about it. Informal gardens fell away
from the house down into the valley, an expanse
of green lawn tempting the eyes and the feet.

The front door of the hotel opened and a man
came towards them.

'Mr Rathby?' he enquired as Luke opened the
car door. 'Your suite is ready for you, sir. Shall I
take up your bags?'

Jenneth was impressed by the attention to detail
that made it possible for Luke to be greeted by
name, and wondered how many guests the hotel
catered for. Probably not very many. It had an air
that suggested it was both discreet and very, very
expensive. She wondered how Luke came to know
about it, and what had made him choose it. It
seemed to breathe peace and tranquillity, and the
kind of privacy she would have thought he most
wanted to avoid.

This was a hotel for lovers, she thought bitterly,
avoiding the hand he stretched out to her as she
got out of the car.

The interior of the hotel was every bit as at-
tractive as the exterior, and in other circumstances
Jenneth would have appreciated the gentle am-
biance of tranquillity reflected by the panelled walls
of the comfortable square foyer.

A smiling receptionist welcomed them and, like
the porter, addressed Luke by his name.

'I'm afraid we don't have a lift,' she apologised
with a smile that included Jenneth. 'Your suite is
on the second floor.'

The stairs rose up to what had once been a min-
strel's gallery, but Jenneth paid scant attention to

the hotel's historical detail, glancing only briefly at the enormous window that dominated the stairs.

It was heavily leaded with various armorial bearings picked out in stained glass, something which normally would have fascinated her, but she was too wrought up to listen when Luke started to explain that the house was built on the site of a much older building.

As she deliberately looked away from him, she thought she saw his mouth compressing slightly, but she ignored it, just as she was determined to ignore him.

He had got what he wanted...a mother for Angelica. Why he had considered it necessary to go through this farce of an honeymoon she had no clear idea at all. It could only be a refined form of purgatory for both of them: Luke because it must remind him of his first wedding...his *first* wife...his *first* honeymoon with the woman he had loved; she because it could only underline the fact that Luke did *not* love her.

Only half a dozen doors opened off the second-floor landing. Luke stopped outside one of them and inserted the key they had been given, standing back to allow Jenneth to precede him inside.

The room was furnished in keeping with the period of the house. Its windows stood open to the small balcony almost opposite the door, and the view beyond.

A suite, the girl on reception had said, and Jenneth had visualised two bedrooms, perhaps connected by a small, dull sitting-room. Instead she was standing in what would have passed for an elegant drawing-room, furnished with two comfortable sofas, a writing desk and chair, a large reproduction cabinet which she guessed probably housed a TV set and a small oval dining-table, large enough to seat four.

The room was decorated in shades of blue and yellow, reflecting the golden sunlight pouring in through the open french windows.

Someone knocked on the door. Luke opened it, and a man came in with their cases.

'I'll put them in the bedroom, shall I, sir?' he asked, and Luke nodded.

It wasn't until Luke had discreetly tipped him and the door had closed behind him that Jenneth realised the potential significance of that word 'bedroom'—in the single.

'A shower, I think, and then possibly dinner, unless you'd prefer to explore the grounds a little first...'

The bland casualness of Luke's remark deflected her concentration and Jenneth stared uncertainly at him.

She must have misunderstood. Luke would never have booked only one bedroom. She was panicking unnecessarily.

'I think I'd like to unpack. How long will we be staying?' she responded.

'Only a couple of days, I'm afraid. I can't take too much time off at the moment. Someone at the hospital recommended this place. Apparently they have a marvellous chef, and a comprehensive range of outdoor activities... riding, fishing in season, tennis, walking, golf.

'I thought we'd have dinner up here tonight. It would give us both time to adjust to our new status...'

He gave her a slightly crooked smile, and because it tugged unbearably at her heartstrings, making her feel as though he was actually daring to pretend that this was as new to him as it was to her, she said bitingly, 'I shouldn't have thought you'd have needed to do much adjusting. After all, it isn't as though this is the first time you've been married.'

She turned her back on him and walked towards the french windows, fiercely blinking away the tears that threatened to betray her. What on earth had possessed her to make such a stupid comment?

'Jenneth...'

She hadn't heard him move, and froze when she felt his hands on her shoulders, shrugging quickly away from him, saying distantly, 'I'll go and unpack...'

And then, hesitating as she crossed the room to the door the porter had disappeared through, she turned back to ask, 'Which is my room?'

There was a long pause while Luke looked at her calmly and thoughtfully before saying evenly, 'It is customary for bride and groom to share a room.'

She withstood his gaze for as long as she could, and then whispered disbelievingly, 'You've only booked one room...?' Betrayed by the emotions seething inside her, the reality of his rejection of her, she demanded huskily, 'Why? For convention? After all, we both know that it isn't because you...'

Inexplicably, the final denouncing words stuck in her throat, refusing to be uttered. Why was it so difficult to say 'it isn't because you desire me'? After all, it was the truth.

Luke, though, didn't seem to share her disability.

'What is it we both know, Jenneth?' he asked her softly, walking towards her. 'What were you going to say? That I don't want you?'

He looked at her without smiling, a look with which she was totally unfamiliar, a brooding male look that made her stomach quiver and heat start to pour through her body.

'Are you really so blind?' he said mockingly.

And, before she could stop him, he had crossed the space that divided them and she was in his arms, his mouth smothering the protests she would have made, his hands moving swiftly and impatiently over her body as he moulded her against him, and for a startled second she felt the hardening evidence of his arousal.

Luke, aroused by *her*? Impossible. And yet the evidence, tangible and erotic, was there. Not just in his arousal, but in the dark flush that burned his skin and the febrile glitter that darkened his eyes.

'I think we'll forget about unpacking and dinner, don't you?' he said softly against her mouth and, before she could deny what he was suggesting, he picked her up and carried her through into the bedroom, kicking the door closed behind him.

It was furnished in the same colours as the sitting-room. Heavy net curtains cast a veil over the sunlight outside, and the smell of beeswax and pot-pourri hung evocatively on the air.

As soon as he put her down on the bed, Jenneth opened her mouth to tell Luke to let her go—to tell him to leave her alone, that she didn't want him; but before she could frame the words he was kissing her, fiercely, savagely almost, bearing her back against the mattress, his movements those of a man gone totally beyond restraint, his voice raw and unfamiliar as he muttered thickly against her mouth that he wanted her...ached for her...needed her so badly.

Before she could stop him, he had unzipped her dress and eased it away from her body.

She shuddered as his hands touched her breasts, fierce, sheeting sensation running through her, her body tightening and coiling in remembered anticipation of the pleasure he had already shown it.

This was crazy...impossible...totally wrong, but as she fought to hold on to that knowledge her body was caught up in the unstoppable surge of a different, older knowledge, and, while she tried frantically to deny what was happening to her with her mind, her body turned traitor on her, and the touch of Luke's mouth burning her skin through the fine silk that covered it brought a haunted moan to her lips and caused her body to arch eagerly into his hands.

This was wrong...wrong...but how could it be when it felt so right...when she ached so much for the possession of Luke's hands...his mouth...his body? When he wanted her, as she had always dreamed of him wanting her? Surely she had the right to take what she was being offered?

'Touch me, Jenneth...I want to feel your hands on me...your mouth...'

His hot breath burned against her ear, his demands fragmented and urgent, making her senses spin dizzily out of control. She reached for him instinctively, obeying the urgent summons of his desire and her own.

He had already discarded his jacket, and she unfastened the buttons on his shirt with impatient, eager fingers, her heart pounding frantically as he impeded her progress by biting the tender flesh of her throat, by cupping her breasts and rubbing his thumbs rhythmically and urgently over her nipples, so that beneath the fine silk of her underwear they peaked and hardened.

When he sat up to shed his shirt he took her with him, his eyes burning hot and dark, never leaving her face, as he dealt swiftly and almost roughly with the removal of his clothes.

As he had pulled her up with him one of the shoulder straps of her teddy had been dislodged. She felt its silken pressure against her arm, and broke the fierce visual contact of his concentration to glance down at it.

Luke's gaze followed hers, too quickly for her to prevent him seeing the rosy darkness of her nipple where it was revealed above the edge of her teddy.

Blushing furiously, she reached for the strap, but Luke stopped her, lowering both his hand and then, with a husky, impatient sound of need, his mouth to the exposed aureole of flesh.

Unprepared for both the intensity of passion generated by the fevered heat of his mouth as he drew fiercely on her sensitive flesh, and her own instinctive reaction to it, she cried out sharply, a low, tormented sound that mirrored the savage stab of sensation that arced through her body and which made Luke hold and taste her almost frenziedly as he responded to its sound.

She had felt desire before, had known what it was like to suffer the unbearable ache of physical need and physical deprivation, but she had never known anything like this . . . had never expected to see Luke held so fast in the grip of that same need that he could not stop himself from compulsively, obsessively almost, caressing every inch of her skin, stroking it, tasting it, arousing it so that she had no ability to even think about resisting him.

His mouth followed the progress of the silky teddy as his hands drew it down her body. When his tongue traced the round indentation of her navel, she moaned and twisted despairingly on the bed, reaching down to curl her hands into his shoulders as, all inhibitions and restraints stripped away, she cried out to him that she couldn't stand what he was doing to her, that her body was going to break apart under the pressure of the fierce need that pulsed inside it.

But her pleas hadn't stopped him, and when at last she lay naked and boneless on the bed, watching him through heavy-lidded, slumbrous eyes, he took her hands and placed them against his own flesh, watching her while he told her how he wanted her to touch him, and she had seen in his eyes the same raw, aching need she knew had been betrayed by her own.

His muscles jerked savagely beneath her stroking fingers, his pores springing sweat that carried his scent and caused her to caress him eagerly with her lips and tongue while Luke trembled and cried out beneath her touch. His hands abruptly reached for her hips, sliding down her thighs and then upwards until he was touching her intimately, learning her and then stroking her, making her cry out with longing and reach blindly for him, needing the sensation of his body within her own so desperately nothing else mattered.

She sobbed with relief as she felt the blissful thrust of him within her, but its relief was short-lived and she craved another and then another, moving with him, accommodating him so that the brief, tearing pang of pain was quickly absorbed and gone, and her body was free to hold him as she had always wanted to hold him, to move with him until the driving urge that possessed them both made her cry out and arch up to him as the tense spiral inside her wound on and on, and the harsh sound of his breathing excited the fierce drumming of her heart. Suddenly the spiral tightened one last time and then exploded into convulsions of such unbearable pleasure that her body shook with the effort of enduring them and tears ran from her eyes. Luke moved, one last, urgent movement that intensified the convulsions to the point where the pleasure was so great that she couldn't quite believe it was real. Luke cried out, a savage, triumphal sound that thrilled her flesh and her spirit, and their bodies shuddered into exhaustion, still gently rocked by echoes of sensation.

'Jenneth ...'

Reluctantly, Jenneth opened her eyes and looked into Luke's.

'You do know why I married you, don't you?' he said huskily, and immediately Jenneth realised what she had done, and her heart and flesh chilled to ice.

'Yes,' she told him curtly, and then, before the misery she could feel burning inside her could betray her any further, she turned her back to him and said bleakly, 'I suppose what just happened *was* necessary, Luke? After all, without it our marriage wouldn't be valid, would it? But I want to make it clear to you that I will never, ever permit it to happen again!'

She felt him move behind her and tensed, dreading having him touch her. He must know that what she was saying was motivated purely by pride... She could understand why he had felt it necessary to ask her if she knew why he had married her. After that uncontrollable way she had reacted to him, he was probably terrified that she had misunderstood his motives. It was different for men; they could feel physical desire without any emotional commitment, and she suspected bitterly that Luke would be quite happy to avail himself of the physical relief her body offered when the need arose, even if at the same time he was making it clear to her that he didn't want any kind of emotional commitment.

'Jenneth ...'

'I don't want to talk about it, Luke,' she told him fiercely. '*You* forced me into this marriage. *I* didn't want it... *I* still don't,' she added acidly.

Only her pride prevented her from asking him who he had been thinking of when he possessed her; if it had been Angelica's mother.

'You wanted me to make love to you...' he reminded her, his voice almost as curt as her own, almost as though she had hurt or offended him in some way, almost as though he was having the same difficulty as she was in controlling his emotions. But that was impossible.

'I'm almost thirty years old, Luke,' she told him, trying to distance herself from what she was feeling and what she knew she had to do. 'You aroused me...I responded.' She shrugged dismissively. 'That doesn't mean that I want to repeat the experience. Oh, and I think it would be as well if you booked another room...'

'I see...' She could hear the hardness in his voice. 'Well, if that's the way you feel...'

'It is,' Jenneth lied shortly.

CHAPTER TEN

THEY had been living together for six weeks. Jenneth had not won her battle for separate rooms, Luke pointing out curtly that to do so would cause questions to be asked by both Angelica and the twins, but he had adhered rigorously to her demand not to touch her, a promise given on the first night of their marriage when she had told him that she would rather sleep outside on the gravel of the hotel car park than share his bed.

In fact, his ready acceptance of her demand that their marriage be non-sexual only confirmed that the desire he had evinced earlier had not really been for her as a person at all.

One morning when Jenneth went to wake up Angelica, she found the little girl complaining that she didn't feel well.

She caught Luke just as he was leaving the house. He frowned as she related Angelica's symptoms and said that he'd go up and have a look at her.

As she waited for his verdict, Jenneth knew that once he had left the house she would not see him again until very late in the evening. Pressure of work was how they explained it to the twins and Angelica, and Jenneth was desperately hoping she could maintain a convincing façade of being happily married at least until the twins had started their university courses.

'There doesn't seem to be anything wrong with her,' Luke pronounced, coming downstairs, frowning slightly. He looked tireder...older, Jenneth acknowledged. Because he regretted what he had done? 'It's probably just the after-effect of too much excitement and ice-cream at yesterday's birthday party.'

A smile curled his mouth, inviting her to share his rueful amusement. She could feel her own mouth softening in response, and fought against the impulse, turning quickly on her heel. She must never allow herself to forget why he had married her...to be deceived into believing that the sadness she sometimes glimpsed in his eyes was caused by their estrangement.

The twins had gone out early; they were spending a few days camping with some friends, so there was no need for her to go through the normal morning farce of kissing Luke's cheek and giving him a loving farewell.

'Jenneth...'

She stopped as she heard the tiredness in his voice, her resolve to treat him as distantly and emotionlessly as she could fragmenting under the pressure of her love for him, but then the telephone rang, and as she went to answer it she heard the front door closing behind him.

When she had finished her phone call she went in to Angelica. The little girl was listless and tetchy, but nothing else appeared to be wrong. Deciding that some fresh air would probably do her good, Jenneth coaxed her into getting dressed, and the two of them went out into the garden.

By lunchtime it was obvious to Jenneth that Angelica was getting worse and not better, and, telling herself that she was probably fussing about nothing, but anxious to make sure, Jenneth bundled her into the car and drove her down to the local surgery.

Dr Hartwell had seen the twins through all their childhood ailments and, while she explained her concern, and Angelica's symptoms, she waited for him to dismiss them kindly as nothing, but he didn't... Instead, he frowned and asked her where Angelica had been recently and with whom, and then after he had examined her he said quietly to Jenneth, 'I'm not sure, but I think there is a possibility it might be meningitis... there's been a small outbreak locally...'

He saw the fear in Jenneth's eyes, and reassured her quickly, 'If it is, we've got it in the very early stages. What I want to do now is get her admitted to hospital for some tests ... I'll give them a ring now. It will be York Memorial.'

'Luke...her father works there...' Jenneth heard herself saying through chattering teeth. 'He's the chief surgeon.'

'Do you think you can drive her in?' Dr Hartwell asked Jenneth as he covered the telephone mouthpiece.

Jenneth nodded. She felt sick with fear and anxiety as she looked into Angelica's flushed little face... *She* had been the one to suggest that Angelica needed company of her own age ... to ask around the village and get Angelica included in the invitations to a couple of birthday parties.

As she waited for Dr Hartwell to warn the hospital to expect them, she tried to envisage telling Luke that she had failed in her responsibility towards his child.

'You say your husband is the chief surgeon... Do you want the hospital to warn him?' Jenneth shook her head. That was *her* responsibility.

Having assured Dr Hartwell that she could manage, she tucked Angelica carefully into the rear seat of her car, wrapping her into the blanket that the surgery had provided and making her as comfortable as she could.

Twice during the journey to York Angelica was miserably and distressingly sick, and by the time the familiar shape of the hospital building came into sight Jenneth's palms were wet where she was gripping the steering wheel, her head pounding with anxious tension.

She drove straight round to the entrance closest to the children's ward, thanking her lucky stars that her work on the mural there meant that she knew exactly where it was, but she was stopped almost as soon as she walked in by a vigilant nurse who explained deftly, relieving her of Angelica's inert weight, 'Isolation, I'm afraid... just until we run some tests and find out exactly what's wrong. It's this way...'

Angelica opened her eyes and said hoarsely, 'My head hurts... I want my Daddy... I want Jenneth...'

Over her head the nurse gave Jenneth a rueful smile. 'Heart-rending, isn't it? But don't worry. She'll be well looked after.'

She was heading for a door marked 'Strictly No Admittance—Isolation Unit'. And Jenneth hurried frantically after her, demanding, 'Can I go with her? I haven't had time to explain to her what's happening...'

'Not just now.' The nurse softened the refusal with an understanding smile. 'It will hold us up if you do, but once we've run the tests, then you'll be able to see her. Try not to worry... I know it isn't easy... I've got two of my own. There's a waiting-room just down the corridor on your left...'

Knowing she was being dismissed, Jenneth lingered just long enough to squeeze Angelica's hand reassuringly and tell her that she was going to be all right.

The little girl seemed not to notice... her eyes were closed, her breathing slightly stertorous.

Jenneth watched the nurse disappear inside the swing doors and then turned blindly down the corridor... it seemed to go on for miles, with no evidence of the waiting-room the nurse had mentioned, and then, abruptly, as she turned a corner it ended with a pair of double doors and a notice saying 'Private'.

As she stood staring at it in confused torpor, the door suddenly swung open and Luke walked through it, accompanied by two other men.

He was talking to one of them, but broke off when he saw Jenneth standing there.

'Jenneth?' he queried sharply.

She looked blankly at him, and he saw the anguish in her eyes and reacted immediately, leaving his companions to go to her, placing his hands on her shoulders and saying firmly, 'Jenneth, what is it? What's wrong?'

He had had to deal with people in shock far too often not to recognise its symptoms now.

'One of the twins?' he hazarded.

Jenneth shook her head, gathering strength from his touch, too grateful for his presence to query how it had happened.

'It's Angelica,' she told him brokenly, barely feeling the sudden bite of his fingers as they tightened on her flesh. 'After you left she seemed to get worse... I took her down to the surgery just after lunch. Dr Hartwell thinks it might be meningitis. They're going to do some tests...'

'Oh, no...'

The raw pain in his voice broke through her own terrified fear. Instinctively she reached out to touch him, wanting to offer him some crumb of comfort, however small.

'Dr Hartwell said that if it was meningitis, we've caught it in the early stages...'

The two men were still standing in the corridor a few feet away; now the more senior of them moved, coming over to them.

'Luke, I'm on my way down to medical now. I'll find out what's going on.'

And in his eyes Jenneth saw the pity he was unable to hide. That terrified her more than anything else. Her heart thumped with panic and pain. Somehow, in Dr Hartwell's surgery, and even here at the hospital, she had been able to take reassurance in the calm unflappability of the people around her... to believe that since Dr Hartwell seemed to suggest that Angelica was not seriously ill, everything was going to be all right... But just for a moment she had seen the stark, unpalatable truth both in Luke's eyes and in those of his colleague.

Luke released her, stepping back from her, just at the same time as the younger man said respectfully, 'The Henderson op, sir...will you want to cancel it?'

Luke had his back to him, and only Jenneth saw the brief betraying gesture, as he spread his hands and looked briefly at their fine tremor, and then said curtly, 'No, he can't afford any delay, his condition's critical enough as it is. If we don't operate today, his blood pressure could drop and it could be days before we can get it up again. Days that he just can't afford. Give me five minutes,' he finished briefly, and as both men's footsteps faded along the corridor, leaving them alone, he returned his hands to Jenneth's shoulders and said huskily, 'I know I don't have to ask you to stay with her, Jenneth... I want to be there, but I can't... not yet...'

'They said they'd let me go to her when they've finished running the tests,' Jenneth told him. 'I was looking for a waiting-room.' She gave him a puzzled frown, shock tearing down the barriers of bitterness and anguish. 'I found you instead...' Tears spurted in her eyes and automatically she put her head on his shoulder.

'It's my fault...she probably got it at the birthday party. Oh, Luke... I'm so sorry...'

'Don't be—and don't blame yourself...'

Incredibly, he was holding her close, stroking the softness of her hair, soothing her with the comfort of his presence.

'I must go...' He released her reluctantly. 'I'll show you the way back to the ward—this place is like a warren.'

Afterwards Jenneth had no idea how long she waited to be summoned back to the ward; time seemed to have no meaning. The waiting-room had no windows, and she had no awareness of time's passing...only of a deep, numbing sense of futility as she prayed inwardly for Angelica's recovery.

When the nurse eventually came back for her, Jenneth tried to stand up, and discovered abruptly that she couldn't.

'It's all right,' she heard the nurse saying kindly from a distance as she tried to move her head and found that she felt obnoxiously ill. 'Stay still for a moment... you fainted... you'll be all right.'

'Angelica...' Jenneth managed to whisper frantically. 'How...?'

The nurse's voice warmed as she reassured Jenneth.

'Your little girl is going to be fine. We're nearly sure it isn't meningitis... we think she had a nasty bout of food poisoning—maybe something she's allergic to. Does she have any food allergies?'

Jenneth frowned—the dizziness was disappearing, but she still felt distinctly light-headed...this time with relief.

'Not as far as I know...'

The nurse gave her an odd look, but Jenneth didn't register it. 'When can I take her home?' she demanded instead.

The nurse smiled.

'Well, not just yet. We'd like to keep her in overnight just to be on the safe side. She's still a rather poorly little girl, and we want to keep a check on her. You can come and see her, though, if you like...'

If she liked...

Angelica was still in the Isolation Unit, looking frighteningly frail and small surrounded by empty beds.

'I was very sick,' she informed Jenneth, giving her a wan smile, 'but I feel heaps better now.'

As Jenneth went to sit down beside her, she said uncertainly to the nurse, 'Would it be possible to let my husband know that she's going to be all right...?'

'We can't interrupt him while he's in surgery, but I think Dr Clarke is going to bleep a message through to him.'

It was gone six o'clock before the hospital finally pronounced that Angelica had indeed had a nasty bout of food poisoning.

'Which probably means she's not going to be the only victim,' the nurse sighed as she told Jenneth. 'We're still keeping her in overnight...just as a precaution.'

'Can I stay?' Jenneth asked urgently.

The nurse looked hesitant, and then suddenly turned her head as the ward door opened and Luke walked in.

'Oh, Mr Rathby, you've come to see your little girl. She's much better now, but asleep. Your wife was just asking if she could stay overnight...'

Luke looked drained of all his normal vitality, and not even the news about Angelica seemed to touch him. Instinctively Jenneth went over to him, touching his wrist lightly, a wordless gesture of instinctive concern.

'Luke, what's wrong?' she asked, immediately looking at Angelica, worrying that she had not been told the truth.

'It's not Angelica,' he told her curtly. The nurse had discreetly gone to the other side of the room.

'Then what is it?' Jenneth pressed.

His eyes flickered and focused on her, empty of all expression other than one of stark, despairing pain.

And then she knew.

'The operation...'

'The operation was a success, but my patient died...' His voice was raw and painful to listen to. 'His heart just couldn't stand up to the strain. Not even forty years old... Damn!' he swore explosively. 'I've just had to see his wife...'

Jenneth looked from Angelica's peacefully sleeping form to Luke's tormented, anguished face, and made a decision born of love and compassion. 'I'm taking you home,' she said gently but firmly. 'Come on.'

At the door, she turned and said hesitantly to the nurse, 'If Angelica wakes up and asks for us...'

'I don't think she will,' the nurse assured her, 'but don't worry. If she does, we'll make sure she's all right.'

Jenneth drove them home, abandoning her own car in favour of Luke's, more dismayed than she wanted him to see by the defeated, despairing way he slumped in his seat.

Once they were home, she guided him into the sitting-room, and impulsively lit a fire in the empty grate. It wasn't cold, but the flames offered a comfort that she knew instinctively he would need.

Leaving him sitting on the sofa, staring into the flames, she hurried into the kitchen, made an omelette large enough for both of them, and then, without knowing why, instead of making coffee as she had intended, she picked up a bottle of wine and a couple of glasses, loading everything on to a trolley.

Luke was in the same position in which she had left him, shoulders bowed, body unmoving.

He turned his head as she walked in, and grimaced as he saw the trolley.

'I don't want anything to eat,' he told her.

'Neither do I,' Jenneth replied calmly. 'but I'm going to, and so are you...'

A suggestion of a smile touched his mouth, and his eyes glinted briefly and familiarly as he derided, 'And you're going to make me...'

'If necessary,' she assured him coolly, ignoring the glinting look, and the sudden kick of sensation in the region of her heart.

It wasn't... He picked up his plate and ate the omelette, eyebrows lifting as he saw the bottle of wine.

'Whose benefit is that for?' he asked her wryly. 'Yours or mine?'

'Mine,' Jenneth admitted frankly, as he poured them both a glass. 'I don't think I could live through another day like today...'

Luke had suffered double her burden... He had lost a patient, and he had had to endure knowing that his child was seriously, even dangerously ill, and that there was nothing he could do to help her; but Jenneth knew instinctively that Luke was the type of person who responded to the needs of others more easily than he responded to his own, although where that knowledge had come from she had no idea.

'I was so frightened, Luke.' she confessed. 'I love Angelica dearly, but she's your child, and...'

'No, she's not.'

The forceful words dropped like stones into a stunned pool of silence while Jenneth stared at him.

He was holding his wineglass, and he gulped deeply from it, turning the glass restlessly between his fingers, not looking at her.

'Luke, what are you saying?' Jenneth demanded shakily. 'Angelica...'

'Is my half-sister, not my daughter...'

He got up abruptly and clumsily. 'Oh, hell, *this* isn't how I wanted to tell you... I had it all planned... A honeymoon, privacy, a quiet dinner... an opportunity for us both to relax, for us to go back and... But it didn't work out that way. The moment I touched you, the moment you looked at me with those big, wondering eyes that said you didn't believe what was happening to me, I blew the whole thing, and suddenly nothing mattered more than holding you in my arms and making love to you. I blew that as well, didn't I? Far from being as rapturously delighted as I was that we were together at last... Far from wanting my love...'

'Your *love*?' Jenneth stood up shakily to face him. 'You never gave me your love, Luke. You gave me your body... your desire... but not your love. I know you only married me because you wanted a mother for Angelica...'

'You *what*?' He caught hold of her, glaring disbelievingly at her. 'What the *hell* are you saying? You know damned well why I married you—and it has nothing to do with Angelica,' he added brutally. 'I married you because I love you, and you know it. I asked you if you knew after we'd made love, and you said yes...'

Jenneth stared at him.

'But I thought...' She bit her lip and sat down shakily. 'Luke, you can't love me,' she said uncertainly. 'You rejected me. You gave another woman your child and married her...'

'No!' he said explosively, and then he reached for her, hauling her to her feet and pulling her into his arms, placing her hand against his fiercely pounding heart. 'Does *that* feel as though I don't love you?' he ground out bitingly, and then, shockingly and even more urgently, he moved deliberately against her, watching the colour burn under her skin as she felt the hard pulse of his flesh. 'Does that?' he derided savagely. 'Oh, Jenneth, you little fool. Of course I love you... I've *always* loved you. Why the hell do you think I lost control the way I did?'

She flushed wildly, totally unable to look at him, managing only to stammer. 'I didn't know...wasn't sure...'

'You mean you thought it was always like that?' he mocked her. 'Well, I suppose it is if you've been

starving for one particular woman the way I've
starved for you—and that one taste of you wasn't
enough. There hasn't been a day when I haven't
woken up aching for you since.'

'You broke our engagement,' she accused. 'You
married someone else...'

'I know. Come and sit down, and I'll tell you all
about it...'

Hesitantly she did so, torn between believing the
sincerity with which he had declared his love for
her and the inescapable truth of the past.

'Angelica is my father's child. During the summer
you and I got engaged, my father was involved in
an affair with one of his patients...'

He caught Jenneth's indrawn gasp of shock and
grimaced. 'Yes, I know—my father was a very weak
and self-indulgent man, Jenneth. I neither liked nor
respected him, but my mother worshipped him. He
was the foundation-stone of her whole world.

'When my father came to me and told me that
he'd got one of his patients pregnant—a young girl
whose parents were threatening to denounce him
publicly and professionally—all I could think of
was what it would do to my mother...

'There had been whispers in the past...discreet
liaisons with other women, during which she'd
somehow managed to cling on to her pride and her
faith, but she'd been stronger then, her health
better. I knew it would destroy her if the news of
what my father had done broke.

'*He* knew it as well, although it wasn't *her* he
wanted to protect, it was himself,' he said with
disgust. 'Initially he'd wanted the girl to have an
abortion, but she wouldn't agree. Her parents were

elderly, very religious and conformist. They wanted their daughter respectably married, their grandchild provided with a father—any father,' he added bitterly. 'My father begged me to help. I told him that it was impossible, that I loved you ... that we were engaged, and that anyway, even if I were free, there was no reason to suppose that Gwen would agree to marry me. But it seemed I was wrong. Gwen was very malleable ... very young and naïve for her age. She had stood out against my father's urgings that she had an abortion, and that had taken all her courage and her strength. When I met her for the first time, she was a very frightened, very defeated girl. Her parents were threatening to expose my father, my mother was dying slowly in front of my eyes and had perhaps at most twelve months to live ... twelve months, when surely she deserved not to have to go through the trauma that would inevitably occur if my father's relationship with Gwen was made public? I was trapped and there was no way out ...'

He looked at her, turning her hand palm over in his lap and studying it blindly, unable to meet her eyes.

'It was the action of an idealistic, idiotic fool, and you don't know how often and how bitterly I regretted it ... Gwen was a burden I didn't want to have to carry. Emotionally she was as totally dependent as my mother was physically dependent. I sacrificed my own happiness for the sake of my mother...that was *my* decision, *my* pain, but I also sacrificed your happiness, Jenneth, and that was something I had no right to do. I was young and too arrogant ... I thought I knew what was best.

'I married Gwen and went to the States full of noble intentions, telling myself that you would soon forget me, that you'd find someone else, wallowing in so much self-pity that I nearly drowned myself in it.

'I made my father swear to stand by my mother...to make her last months happy and contented.

'She seemed to accept my reason for marrying Gwen, although sometimes since I've wondered... I suspect she thought that Gwen was an aberration, a physical itch I scratched and, having scratched to some effect, had to stand by. I don't think for a moment she guessed the real reason I married her, but I know she knew I loved *you*.

'It was a crazy thing to do...now, with hind-sight, I see I should have approached the Medical Board privately, explained the situation, got help from people far more qualified than I was myself. As it was...

'As it was, once Gwen realised that I wasn't going to be a rock for her to cling to...once she realised that the punishing hours I was working in the States, while I tried desperately to get you out of my mind, meant that we had no time together...once she re-alised that our marriage meant separate bedrooms and separate lives, she looked around for someone else to cling to...and found someone.

'Angelica was eighteen months old when she told me she was leaving me... My mother was dead and, God forgive me, the first thing I felt was relief...relief and the realisation that I could come back and tell you...but then Gwen was killed in a car accident, and when I did come back it was to find that you were indifferent towards me...that your life was full of other things ...other men...' His mouth twisted, and Jenneth felt pity and regret touch her heart as she remembered that Christmas when he had appeared so unexpectedly to taunt her with the evidence of his love for another woman in the shape of his child. 'I was jealous,' she said simply, 'I wanted to hate you and to hate Angelica, but I couldn't.'

She couldn't find the words to say what was in her heart, to tell him how she felt. The events he had just described were so typical of him; had she been older, more knowledgeable, surely she might have guessed at the truth?

'You could have told me,' she said without reproach, but her eyes were shadowed with the pain she had known.

He shook his head. 'Not without begging you to wait for me, asking you for promises I had no right to. I wanted to set you free properly, Jenneth... Or at least I told myself I did. I was too selfishly wrapped up in my own self-pity. We both have our wounds, and I can never forget that I've caused yours, while my own were self-inflicted. I thought you'd forget me and find someone else.'

'I couldn't,' she told him softly, trembling at the look she could see in his eyes.

'Was it because of me that you wouldn't let any other man make love to you?' he whispered against her mouth, and beneath the apparent arrogance of the demand she sensed his deep need and pain, and whispered back,

'Yes.' She felt him shudder in reaction to the movement of her mouth and to her admission. 'I wanted you to be my lover, Luke, only you.'

He shuddered again and said rawly, 'That Christmas I came home hoping against hope that I'd be able to find a way of winning you back. Instead I discovered that you had no interest in me whatsoever...that there were apparently other men in your life. I felt I'd been given a death blow. I told myself that I had no right to feel jealous, to reproach you, but my reactions to the discovery that I'd lost you showed me just how much I'd deceived myself with my supposed nobility. I hated losing you like hell. It was torment...agony...and even then I couldn't stop myself from getting every scrap of information about you that I could from Louise and her parents.

'Everything seemed to have gone wrong for me; my career was prospering, but I had lost the woman I loved, and I had to carry the burden of feeling responsible for my wife's death. If she hadn't married me...'

Jenneth was unable to stop herself from reaching out and touching him compassionately. 'We all have free will,' she reminded him tenderly.

He caught hold of her hand and pressed it to his lips, his mouth burning hot against her skin.

'Yes,' he agreed thickly. 'But I took away your right to use yours when I broke our engagement without telling you the truth. Even when I thought I'd lost you, I still couldn't prevent myself from giving in to the temptation of taking this job in York, a final, last-ditch attempt to get back into your life—and then I stood beneath Louise's bedroom window and miraculously, unbelievably I heard you saying that you still loved me. But saying it in such a way, with such pain and bitterness, that I knew that I couldn't simply rush upstairs, take you in my arms and tell you that I loved you too. You'd erected so many barriers against me, and with good reason.

'I had to plan a campaign...a campaign to make myself a part of your life, and then to tell you the truth once I had a fair chance of being heard. What happened the night before I announced our engagement was not part of that plan,' he assured her huskily. 'The trouble was that I'd tried so hard to resist the temptation of holding you, or loving you, that when I was tempted to use the advantage fate was giving me when Angelica walked in and saw us, I had no resistance left.

'I know now that you love me,' he said unsteadily. 'But can you forgive me, Jenneth; can you admit me back into your life?'

She took a deep breath and then said shakily, 'Yes! I *do* understand why you did it, Luke, and what you did *was* right,' she admitted with painful honesty. 'Your poor mother...' She gave a tiny shudder.

'Can we put the past behind us, Jen?' he asked her quietly. 'Can we start again, building on the foundations of our love...building a relationship strong in trust and truth?'

'Yes!' she whispered, above the fierce pounding of her heart.

'Oh, Jenneth.' He gave a groan as he took her in his arms. 'I've needed you so much.'

Against his ear she whispered softly, 'Love me, Luke. Love me now for all the times you haven't been here for me through the years.'

And, as he obeyed her whispered demands, she heard him telling her over and over again that he loved her, until the words ran through her blood like the pulse of life itself, and she gave herself up joyously and trustingly into the mutual bondage of their love.

THIS JULY, HARLEQUIN OFFERS YOU THE PERFECT SUMMER READ!

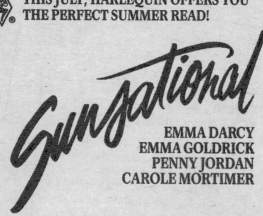

**EMMA DARCY
EMMA GOLDRICK
PENNY JORDAN
CAROLE MORTIMER**

From top authors of Harlequin Presents comes
HARLEQUIN SUNSATIONAL, a four-stories-in-one
book with 768 pages of romantic reading.

Written by such prolific Harlequin authors as Emma Darcy,
Emma Goldrick, Penny Jordan and Carole Mortimer,
HARLEQUIN SUNSATIONAL is the perfect summer
companion to take along to the beach, cottage, on your
dream destination or just for reading at home in the warm
sunshine!

Don't miss this unique reading opportunity.

Available wherever Harlequin books are sold.

Coming soon
to an easy chair near you.

FIRST CLASS is Harlequin's armchair travel plan for the incurably romantic. You'll visit a different dreamy destination every month from January through December without ever packing a bag. No jet lag, no expensive air fares and *no* lost luggage. Just First Class Harlequin Romance reading, featuring exotic settings from Tasmania to Thailand, from Egypt to Australia, and more.

FIRST CLASS romantic excursions guaranteed! Start your world tour in January. Look for the special **FIRST CLASS** destination on selected Harlequin Romance titles—there's a new one every month.

NEXT DESTINATION:
FLORENCE, ITALY

 Harlequin Books

JTR7

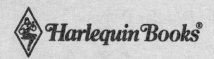
Harlequin Books®

GREAT NEWS...
HARLEQUIN UNVEILS NEW SHIPPING PLANS

For the convenience of customers, Harlequin has announced that Harlequin romances will now be available in stores at these convenient times each month*:

Harlequin Presents, American Romance, Historical, Intrigue:

>   May titles: April 10
>   June titles: May 8
>   July titles: June 5
>   August titles: July 10

Harlequin Romance, Superromance, Temptation, Regency Romance:

>   May titles: April 24
>   June titles: May 22
>   July titles: June 19
>   August titles: July 24

We hope this new schedule is convenient for you.

With only two trips each month to your local bookseller, you'll never miss any of your favorite authors!

*Please note: There may be slight variations in on-sale dates in your area due to differences in shipping and handling.

HDATES-R